The Hotel Next Door

ELIZABETH COOKE

abbott press

Abbott Press books may be ordered through booksellers or by contacting:

Abbott Press
1663 Liberty Drive
Bloomington, IN 47403
www.abbottpress.com
Phone: 1-866-697-5310

Because of the dynamic nature of the Internet, any web addresses or
links contained in this book may have changed since publication and
may no longer be valid. The views expressed in this work are solely those
of the author and do not necessarily reflect the views of the publisher,
and the publisher hereby disclaims any responsibility for them.

The Hotel Next Door is a work of fiction. Names, characters,
places and incidents are the product of the author's imagination
or are used fictitiously. Any resemblance to actual events, locales,
or persons, living or dead, is entirely coincidental.

ISBN: 978-1-4582-1850-6 (sc)
ISBN: 978-1-4582-1851-3 (hc)
ISBN: 978-1-4582-1852-0 (e)

Library of Congress Control Number: 2015900085

Printed in the United States of America.

Abbott Press rev. date: 1/30/2014

PROLOGUE

Where the Shortest Farewells are the best,
The Longest Hellos are the Sweetest.

I will be able to:
Embrace Ludwig Turner, artist and lover, my Brit,
Schmooze with Jean-Luc and Isabella,
Listen to Duke Pierre Davis' music,
Dine with Pierre and Elise Frontenac,
Pose for Sasha Goodwin, photographer *extraordinaire*,
Laugh with Ray Guild,
Gossip with dear friend, Sue de Chevigny,
Solve mysteries with police detective, René Poignal.

Presumably Kurt Vronsky and Jillian Spenser are still in jail.
Surely Emile LaGrange is dead, *bien sûr*.

Quite a roster of characters to return to. Quite a new live history to be written. And what new persons will appear to whet the appetite for discovery? Secrets to disclose? Mysteries to solve?

How utterly thrilling!

As long as Brit is still there for me,
As long as Isabella and Jean-Luc still live *la vie en rose,*
As long as Sasha photographs the rich and famous,
As long as Sue's château still leaks in the rain,
As long as *Caviar Kaspia* provides the best sturgeon roe in the world,
As long as The Hotel Next Door, The Majestic, has the richest clientele in all of Paris,
As long as Hotel Marcel provides the true Paris experience,

I will know that the *Tour Eiffel* still reigns,
And I will be ecstatic.

CHAPTER ONE

J'Arrive!

IT'S CHRISTMAS TIME.

It's Paris time—and what a 'present' to myself to be here!

The Eiffel Tower wears a thin coat of translucent ice. As the weak sun melts it down throughout the day, it leaves a puddle at the base of each of the iron feet. At night, the tower glistens.

I am here again in my favorite place—the Hotel Marcel—with Jean-Luc Marcel, the owner, presiding at the front desk in the miniscule lobby. I am here again to enjoy the pure Parisian ambiance of this small hotel, and the company of friends I have encountered on previous visits, the most recent one being last May.

What a way to spend Christmas!

Who needs a turkey when there is roast partridge? Who needs eggnog when *Champagne* appears in a flute? Who needs pumpkin pie when there are macaroons, all crispy and sweet, to enjoy?

The other is very nice—very homey—but in Paris, although it is still very much Christmas, there is an understated, romantic atmosphere.

The glorious monuments are lighted at night. The tour boats on the Seine are decorated with greenery, and The Eiffel Tower gleams with diamonds in the darkness as the toll of church bells fills the city of Paris with music.

Christmas time in Paris. Unforgettable. *Inoubliable!*

From my little room on the fifth floor of Hotel Marcel, I can step out on my balcony and gaze again at the three apartments that, in the past, have provided such entertainment. Like miniature stages, each has presented true life-crises of the most intense kind. Even murder.

Now, on this Friday of my arrival, this evening, as dusk descends, from my balcony I can see in apartment building 1, the apartment of the now widow Sylvie Vronsky LaGrange. The blinds are open, and the salon is lighted. There is a small Christmas tree in the corner, and although the widow is not in the room, the whole place is transformed, from rather pedestrian furnishings, to those of grand luxe!

My goodness. Sylvie has surely changed her spots. The sofa is velvet. There is a chandelier hanging from the ceiling, and a large gold framed mirror on the far wall. A new, red leash for Schnitzel, the dog, hangs by the salon door. I wonder who walks him now, since Sylvie's brother Kurt who used to have that duty, is in jail because he killed her husband, Emile LaGrange. *Quel drame.*

Into the fifth floor apartment of building 2, I can see nothing because silk drapes cover the large front windows. Who lives there now? It was Sasha Goodwin's duplex last year. Then Jillian Spenser, the British artist/forger, also now in jail, lived there with her young daughter, Amelia, but who now? I must find out from Jean-Luc.

The fifth floor of apartment building 3 where the Frontenacs reside, is also closed from view, with damask curtains covering any possibility of seeing inside. Does Pierre Frontanac's illegitimate African-American son, Duke Pierre Davis, live with them? *Quelle situation!* I would doubt it although, *en fin,* they—even the wife, Elise,—accepted him as their own. What a fine young musician is Duke Davis. I must go hear him again at *Le Club,* the jazz *boïte* where he found a job as bass player.

Saving the best for last, as I close the French doors to the balcony and prepare for bed, I think of Brit. He had been with me in New

York for a week in October. We were inseparable and close, intimate, companionable. His leaving was wrenching, but there was always Paris to look forward to at Christmas, the paramount reason for my being here.

Yet, when he left New York to cross the Atlantic, I felt let down, bereft. I still knew him not at all—in a way—his persona opaque and mysterious. What did I expect of him? At this age, me in my 60s, he close behind, just where do I think this will lead? What do I want from our couple-hood?

I am soon to get an answer of sorts, and one I do not want to hear.

CHAPTER TWO

Brit

IT IS FRIDAY night, a week before Xmas.

We had New York in October—lovely golden days and nights under cool, midnight skies.

Now I am once more in Paris…as arranged, earlier this fall, to meet again, at Christmas time in The City of Light, to be together, where 'Diamants en Pluie,' 'Diamonds in the Rain,' that beautiful expression of love he painted at the beginning of our romance, had been inspired! In this very room.

I am to call him at his studio/apartment in the Marais on my arrival at Hotel Marcel.

Now I do just that, my first night in town.

A woman answers.

"Who's this?" I ask.

"Marianna," is the reply. Then silence. "Who's this?" she asks, her voice hostile, suspicious.

In shock, I hang up. Marianna! His old lover?

I thought she had drowned. Brit had told me so, that she had committed suicide by walking out into the ocean, off the beach in Southern California.

And I believed him.

What? What? I think. Was his tale of past love a lie? Was Marianna's death a fable, and if so, why? I have taken all he has said on faith. I have loved him true.

And Ray Guild, my editor friend at *Vogue*. He would be as perplexed as I. Ray had told me of Marianna's untimely demise. He had warned me, in his own ironic way, that Brit had a beleaguered past, that there was mystery to his early years

Yet, Marianna! Back in his home! Oh God, this is hard to bear.

I guess I have the answer after all. It's one I cannot accept easily. It's an answer that brings tears on this beautiful night in Paris. All hope... for what? For the love I expected, for one that I dreamed of, that trust seems lost in the smoke of deceit.

It's over, I think, as a curl on my side on the bed, legs drawn to my chest, cheek on a pillow that quickly turns wet with tears.

CHAPTER THREE

'Fusion'

THERE IS A knock on my door around 8:00 o'clock. It is Isabella, asking me to join her and Jean-Luc at the bar of The Majestic, the new hotel next door, for a welcoming celebration drink on my return to Paris. Jean-Luc has told me that this grand place is owned by a conglomerate in Qatar.

I cannot say no, and hurriedly, I patch myself together, telling her I will be right downstairs in moments. With a quizzical expression on her face, Isabella leaves me to repair the damage of the 'Marianna' phone call.

Jean-Luc, Isabella and I are sitting at a small, round black table in the bar of The Majestic Hotel next door, called The Maj, by some of the locals. We are drinking a *Pinot Noir*, under the tented ceiling, as the small lamp with red fringe—one on each table—lights our faces.

The ambiance is exotic, different, and all three of us feel out of place, uncomfortable. I have decided to treat this meeting as a welcome distraction for my sorrowful heart. I force myself to smile as often as possible.

The bar is quite crowded with a sophisticated group of people—Asians, an Oriental pair at a corner table, several French persons, and directly next to where we are sitting is an American couple, so obviously American, it is embarrassing.

The two are both plump, pink-faced and self-satisfied looking. His voice is as loud as is his Christmas sweater, with its bright red and green reindeer motif. His laugh resounds. She sits there complacently—I can hear him call her Madge—which brings a large dimple in each of her cheeks as she smiles. And from her, one listens to her very Southern, 'Yes, Jerry honey. Yes, Jerry sweetie' as she responds to her noisy husband.

Out of the blue, I see Madge give me a little wave and mouthe the word 'American?' with a conspiratorial nod. I turn away chagrinned, sorry I am as obviously identifiable as American as are they. I feel hardly up to any gregarious interaction, least of all Jerry and Madge from the deep South, unless its dear friends like Jean-Luc and Isabella.

Suddenly Jean-Luc is on his feet. "*Un moment*," he says softly, and leaves us at the table.

"Hmm." I am curious.

"What is he up to?" says Isabella, but we see him crossing the lobby with its black and white tile floor, and he quickly rejoins us at the bar.

In his hand is the menu from the '*Fusion*' dining room. He proceeds to read to us, from the enormous black leather bound list of entrees, appetizers, desserts.

"Listen: 'Coucous with dried currants, pistachios in sauce nutmeg.'" Jean-Luc is translating from the French for my benefit.

"Look at the price!" Isabel exclaims, leaning over his shoulder. "28 euros…for the cheapest grain in the whole world."

"And no meat," Jean-Luc says. "How about 'Golden shrimp *au printemps* with jicama sticks, peas, broccoli *florets*, asparagus tips in ginger *vinaigrette?*'"

"Ouch", I say.

Isabella is laughing uncontrollably. "For Jean-Luc, who is master chef, this is too much."

"Oh, and of course there are pages of sushi choices," he continues. "They have a famous Japanese chef, *évidemment*, or so it says here."

"What about poor old *coq au vin*, or *soufflé au fromage*, or *boeuf bourguignon?* things French," I remark vehemently.

"Aha, Madame Elizabeth. That is it! That's where I have the advantage—the Hotel Marcel does—not that I have a restaurant *chez moi*—but I offer *une ambiance vraiment française*, something that The Maj cannot!"

Bien sûr," I say, with as much conviction as I can muster...with a broken heart.

CHAPTER FOUR

Duplex, Building 2, Fifth Floor

WE THREE ARE still at the bar of The Majestic Hotel on this Friday night of my arrival. I am determined to remain interested in life, even as my expectation of love seems to have been crushed. So I ask Jean-Luc about the duplex across the street that Sasha had occupied, followed by the art forger, Jillian Spenser, now incarcerated. "Is anyone living there now?"

"Indeed. The actual owners have moved in."

"Really. Who are they? Do you know them?"

"*Absolument.* Henri and Louise Croix. He is a diplomat. I believe he was the French Ambassador in Ethiopia for some years. He's an interesting fellow. Louise is…how do you say…"

"*Excentrique?*" Isabella interjects.

Jean-Luc laughs. "*Oui,* you could say so. Surely, she is an original."

"How so? I ask.

"I think she's kind of spooky, you know, with black, black hair and bluish-red lipstick." Isabella grimaces.

"A bit of a witch?" I say with a laugh.

"Exactly! She is bizarre…mysterious. She talks in a very low voice of things occult, about the rituals she witnessed in their time in Africa," Jean-Luc intercedes.

"You sound as if you know her well, Jean-Luc."

When I say this, I notice that he glances slyly at Isabella.

"*Eh bien*, I guess I do. I have known her for years—before her marriage—she had a shop with very strange artifacts from all over the world. It was not very successful, but then she married Edouard. And now, well, I might as well tell you, but it's something of a secret, I am seeking to buy the apartment. They are staying there only until a house they purchased in a village near the Fontainebleau Forest is renovated. Then they plan to sell the duplex, or if they can't, re-lease it again."

"You want to buy the apartment?" I am surprised.

"And why not," he says, looking at a smiling Isabella. "Yes, I want to buy it. It's a great building. All three of those buildings across the street were built in 1928, very Art Deco which I love. And there's a parking garage on the side, which could provide parking for Hotel Marcel. Also, there are two separate elevators in the building, the back one for servants, in the old style. That's the way they did it in the past…kept the servants separate."

"Yes, I remember," I say. "That's the way Kurt got to his brother-in-law's bedroom—to kill him—by the back elevator. Of course, he had a key to the apartment to let himself in because he was always walking sister Sylvie's dog, Schnitzel. Yes, I remember—and the attic room where he lived above them."

"Speaking of that, the attic room in building 2 is now rented to guess who?"

"I have no idea," I reply. "Sasha?"

"No, not Sasha. Duke Davis!"

"Duke? Really? I am truly pleased. "I so like Duke," I say, "I really like him a lot, and I love his music. Is he still playing at *Le Club*?"

"*Bien sûr.* In fact, he is quite the headliner."

"I must go hear him play."

"Yes, " says Isabella. "We'll all go. But about the apartment…there's a large kitchen with a double oven Cornu stove with a gas top for Jean-Luc's cooking, and there's a balcony over the street with red carnations, and…"She is bubbling, animated.

"How fabulous," I say.

"Fabulous is right," Jean-Luc says with a rueful grin.

"The Price! Now that's really fabulous!"

"Dare I ask the amount?" I inquire tentatively.

"One million nine-hundred thousand euros."

"Wow."

"Yes. Wow! But we're haggling."

"I didn't realize you planned to leave your apartment over the *pharmacie.*"

"Well, it has just sort of come about. I love this avenue. I love the hotel, and the neighborhood. It will be perfect when I retire across the street in that apartment. I can cook my *choucroute garnie*, and watch my small hotel from my balcony. I'll be, as you say in America, up close and personal!" Jean-Luc beams a great smile, leans across the table and kisses Isabella.

Aha, I think. I see a future in mind, for the two of them.

I think of the Gershwin song. "They're writing songs of love but not for me. Although I can't dismiss, the memory of his kiss, I guess he's not for me."

Not for me. Dammit, Brit.

CHAPTER FIVE

Phone Tag

DUKE IS IN the attic room of apartment building 2, above the duplex belonging to Henri and Louise Croix, the apartment Jean-Luc is in the process of buying. How appropriate, I think. Duke is now one building away from his father, Pierre Frontenac—in apartment building 3—and directly across from his friends on the opposite side of the street, one of whom is me.

It is Saturday morning. I pick up my binoculars, a present from Jean-Luc a couple of visits ago when he found I was 'a little spy on the fifth floor.' He had been intrigued with this, hence the gift –'to make it easier.'

Out on the balcony in the cold freshness of an early day in December, I peer across the quiet avenue at the door to Duke's room at the top of building 2, a door that is divided in half, the top, when open, being the only window into the place. Right now, it is shut.

I return to my room, despondent, not from Duke's shuttered door—I would soon find him—but from having no contact with Brit. He has not called. Did that Marianna person tell him a woman had phoned? If so, did he assume it was me, and wonder how I might react to a female voice answering the phone in his tiny apartment?

I certainly have no intention of calling again, although I am aching to hear his voice. I hate how I need him.

But Marianna!

What excuse can he give? Marianna indeed. He can't get out of this one, and the hideous story of abortion, miscarriage, and suicide. What kind of man would create this lie to someone he cared about?

If he cared.

Well, it was nice while it lasted

No, it was beautiful, but then there is no fool like an old one.

The phone rings. I answer.

"Elizabeth?"

It is his voice and I slam down the receiver.

The phone rings again. I let it peal away. I decide I am not going to answer any phone calls, none at all.

It rings a third time, but only sounds twice. Then all is silent.

I sit on the edge of the bed, totally deflated. Here I am in my beloved Paris, acting the fool. I decide this is silly. Jean-Luc, Sasha, Sue de Chevigny, Ray Guild—old friends. I want to speak to them always.

I will answer the phone from now on. Should it be Brit on the other end, I will somehow know how to react to this man who fled to Paris to escape his past.

Or so it seems.

CHAPTER SIX

Sunday

HAMAD AL-BOUDI ARRIVES at The Majestic Hotel, the hotel next door. My balcony is on the same level as the nearest royal suite of The Majestic so it feels I can practically touch it, although there is another small balcony of Hotel Marcel next to mine in between.

It is late Sunday morning, and as I look out across the avenue, down below to the right, I see a white, stretch limousine, arrive, discharging first, two bodyguards in black suits, then Hamad al-Boudi himself in flowing robes, (I find out his name later from Jean-Luc,) followed by four women in burkas, top to toe, with veils covering their lower faces, only eyes peering out. One seems much younger than the three leading, heavier women who run after the emir (if he is actually one so eminent.)

The younger, more slender one, lingers, looks about with her fine, brown eyes, even spots me on my balcony. I can tell she sees me. Her eyes seem to lighten. She quickly appraises the small Hotel Marcel, as she is summoned by a bodyguard to enter The Majestic, which she does with a backward glance.

It is cold out here on the balcony, but before I return to the warmth of my room, I look across to apartment building 1 and into Sylvie's fifth floor apartment salon where I see she is entertaining a silver-haired gentleman. (Her dead husband, Emile LaGrange, had similar hair. Hmm. No wonder this man appeals to her.)

Sylvie is semi-reclining on the sofa, in a lacy white peignoir, her bobbed red hair close to the face, in full make-up, and from her body language, I can tell she is being extremely coy. The man sits across from her in an elaborate easy chair, one leg crossed over his knee. Each has a coffee cup in hand.

Well, well, I think. Another new character on this street of dreams. The man looks familiar. Aha! He looks like the doctor who arrived the day after Emile LaGrange was killed, to treat the new widow's hysterics. Yes indeed, I decide. That IS the good doctor himself.

Sylvie certainly works fast.

CHAPTER SEVEN

Dr. Guillaume Paxière

IT LOOKS LIKE Dr. Paxière is Sylvie's new lover—silver haired, dapper, not a bad doctor, but a con artist when he smells money. I can tell, even at this distance, and with the help of binoculars, that Dr. Guillaume Paxière likes the lushness of the LaGrange apartment with its handsome furniture and crystal chandelier.

He has many such *liaisons*, retains a veritable little black book of available (rich) older females who he services, not only with medicines, but with his well-toned body. I know from experience, because this good doctor is a person I met some years ago on a previous visit!

I had rejected him from the beginning, when we met at a cocktail *soirée* given by Ray Guild, my friend and editor of French *Vogue*, five years ago. Dr. Paxière, a widower, had come on to me strong, so obvious it was almost laughable. But I had agreed to have dinner with him.

Over the table in a chic restaurant near the Étoile, I discover that he lives the life of an aging *boulevardier*, cynical but charming, knowledgeable of Paris' pleasures, and only too ready to supply a little 'loving' to a hungry partner, which, apparently, he does frequently.

Now Sylvie is the object for his seduction. Recently widowed, obviously wealthy, and not too unattractive, to Dr. Guillaume Paxière she is fair game, and eager to be 'taken advantage of.' How he loves to drag out the procedure, until the female is ravenous for his affection, and he knows all too well just how to prolong her agony (and final ecstatic fulfillment.)

God bless him. Dr. Paxière is classic! Poor Sylvie doesn't have any idea who she's dealing with. And she doesn't have a chance.

I caught onto his game, early and fast. He was quite livid when I told him some home truths about himself, those five years ago. In fact, I know he is not the kind of man to forgive a woman for 'calling him out.' He is a man, however, who cannot forget his resentment. In fact he clings to it, enjoys the feeling of being wronged.

Good Lord, I hope we don't by chance meet on the street. If we should, I'll merely say, *bonne chance*, and bye-bye.

Now Sylvie? That's another story. I cannot warn her. She already hates me. Our history of the jailing of her brother Kurt, with me as witness to his wrongdoing; of her husband's obsession with my friend, Isabella, and his subsequent murder; my allegiance with Sasha, the photographer, who plagued brother Kurt by taking his reluctant picture; all this made for truly bad blood towards me. I guess I can't blame her.

Besides, she would never believe me. She is obviously in Dr. Paxière's seductive thrall.

CHAPTER EIGHT

Sue

"MARIANNA, EH. MAYBE she's his daughter," Sue announces.

We are at our favorite haunt, *Caviar Kaspia*, for their sumptuous caviar/vodka lunch, my first Monday in Paris.

"Can't be his daughter. Brit says he never wanted children, that his paintings are his 'legacy.' He even had a vasectomy. He was adamant, particularly after Marianna's death…if she is dead," I say woefully.

"Come on, kiddo. Give him a break. He told you she died," Sue admonishes. "Don't rush to question everything."

"Then who the hell is this woman—this new Marianna? That's not such a usual name, you know," I say belligerently.

"Well, don't get mad at me," Sue says.

"I'm sorry. But how could he lie like that and make up such a horrible story of her walking out into the ocean and continuing until she drowned…on purpose."

"There you go! Stop it. Please, darling, try to find out the truth before you treat him like some sort of criminal," says Sue, swallowing the last of her vodka.

Suddenly, Sue makes me feel so judgmental, so quick to jump to conclusions before knowing all the facts. I feel so unkind, so uncompassionate, so willing to think the worst of a man I have come to love. Forgive me, Brit. I know not what I do.

And yet?

"What if the woman who answered was named Margot or Gloria or Jezebel? Would that have been worse?" Sue quizzes me.

"God, I don't know. That would have been pretty bad—to think he had a 'squeeze' living with him. But his lies would be new, not some specter from the past raising its head to haunt me."

"Now you are being dramatic," Sue says, not unkindly. "Honestly, I can't blame you either way- I know how fond you are of this handsome artist, that you've had great times with him."

"Yes, and so unexpected at this time of my life."

"Ah, sweetheart, one is never too old to dream," Sue says with a sigh. "I don't mean to be hard on you. Perhaps I'm a little jealous."

"Not you, Sue, not you."

"In any case, I think you have to pursue it."

"How do you mean?"

"You have to give another call."

"I can't."

"Of course you can. You must. Then maybe you can put this whole lie thing to rest. If he has been lying, well, you'll know. You can cut the head off the snake, so to speak. For your own sake. And if, by chance, there is a real reason there's a Marianna in his house, then you'll know that too and will either accept it or not. At least there'll be an end to the quandary."

"And I can get some sleep."

"Hey, you're here to enjoy Paris. Don't let this spoil it for you." And Sue leans forward and pats me gently on the shoulder. "You've always got me and caviar and Jean-Luc and the dramatic goings on across the street."

"And at The Majestic," I say brightening. "What a ridiculous place, oh, maybe not ridiculous, but it is outlandish in a way. I saw another emir arrive yesterday in a white limousine with bodyguards and four burka-clad females—actually one of them looked to be young. I tell you, if a woman in a burka can look lithe, this young one did. And she had amazing, huge dark eyes…really quite striking for a woman completely covered."

"Ah, a new character for you to 'binocularize.'"

I laugh. "But of course! How could I not? She must be a daughter of the emir, that Arab potentate."

"Is he really the emir?"

"I have no idea. I just call him that."

"I can see you're headed for trouble,"

Sue says with a laugh and a toast to me with her vodka glass. "As usual!"

CHAPTER NINE

A Girl Called Lilith

DUKE DAVIS HAS come across the street from his attic room in apartment building 2 to enjoy a late breakfast with me in the salon this Tuesday morning. We are catching up on our lives, his, happy and fulfilling, his musical future secure at least for now, and, most of all, his relationship with his father, strong.

"It's a bit different with Elise. I never know what to call her," he says hesitantly. "I can't call her…mom…or step-mom…but she has been nice enough to me, and I'm grateful she gives me access to my father." Duke beams. "He comes a lot to *Le Club*."

"That's wonderful, Duke," I respond.

Then, I see Duke's world turn upside down, as he watches a young woman rush into the lobby of the Hotel Marcel. She is fully covered in the dark clothing of the Arab woman, her face veiled, and the large, brown eyes, with their winged brows, come to rest on Duke.

For whatever reason, Duke has risen to his feet.

"Please, sir, may I use a lavatory?" the young woman breathes in

French, as she approaches Jean-Luc behind the check-in desk. Her accent sounds almost British, as she looks over her shoulder and out the lobby door, obviously in some distress.

"*Mais, oui,* Mademoiselle" Jean-Luc replies graciously. "There is a *salle de bain, en bas…* downstairs." he continues in English.

"Oh," she says. "You speak English. That is better for me."

Jean-Luc comes around the desk and takes her to the small circular stairway to the basement, Duke mesmerized by the scene. Below, it has been refurbished, with not only piping improvements for the building and a new mechanism for the elevator, but there is a small bedroom and bath, where Antoine, the student-night-man at the desk of the hotel, naps. Even Jean-Luc has been known to stay there during renovations and emergencies, although rarely.

"Down to your right, Mademoiselle," he says, and she quickly, with light steps, descends. He peers after her and then joins us at the breakfast table.

"More *café?*" he says, lifting the pot, at which I nod and he pours the fragrant liquid into my oversized cup.

"She must have come from next door," I say in a whisper. As I do, two dark-suited, tough-looking men enter the hotel. Jean-Luc rises to greet them.

In French, he asks if he can help them.

In gruff tones, the older fellow inquires if he has seen a young Arabic lady, at which Jean-Luc shakes his head, "Here?" the other man asks, "or on the street outside?" Still, Jean-Luc nods a 'no.' The older man turns to the other and says contemptuously, "She'd never come into a place like this," and the two leave in a rush.

With a grim smile, Jean-Luc returns to our table.

"Thank goodness she is taking a long time," I say.

"Do you suppose she's hiding from those bodyguards?"

"I would say so," says Duke. "I hope she's OK down there. Do you think you should go down and see if she's all right?"

"I'll give her another minute," I say.

"Those *bâtards!*" Jean-Luc mouthes under his breath. For some reason, Jean-Luc feels at war with The Hotel Majestic.

"You really can't stand what's going on next door," I declare, with a little smile.

"You're right. The whole place is pretentious… so un-French!" His strong feelings make Jean-Luc more than eager to come to the succor of a young 'emir's' daughter, resident of The Majestic, if that is what the new little stranger is. Suddenly, he says "Perhaps, Elizabeth, it's best if you go and look after her?"

"You're right. I'll see what's cooking," I say, and off I go to the stairway and down the steps.

Once in the new, pristine white hall next to the bedroom, I knock on the bathroom door. "Are you okay?"

"*Oui.*"

"Do you need help?"

"*Non.*" And the door opens. The young girl emerges. She is wearing a long gray skirt and short black wool jacket, tight to her body, a chador partially covering hair, which is sleek as satin, straight, and the color of ebony. She has olive skin, and the whitest teeth, which are emphasized by the white hair covering.

She is breathtakingly pretty.

As we walk upstairs, me first, carrying the dark burka and face veil, both remarkably heavy and smelling of perfume, she tells me her name is Lilith.

I respond by announcing mine. Elizabeth.

As we reach the lobby, I hear Duke, his head lifted, mouth slightly open, emit an audible sigh.

Well, strike one for our new girl, Lilith! I can see for a fact that Duke is completely taken by her beauty, and I can hardly blame him. I know, too, that if sheik Hamad al-Boudi actually is her father, she will have trouble in Paris with this turn of events. Big trouble.

And so will Duke!

CHAPTER TEN

To Shed A Burka

JEAN-LUC GOES TO meet Lilith at the top of the stairs. He takes the burka and veil from my hands. "Mademoiselle, would you like a *café?*" She nods shyly.

"*Au lait?*"

"*Oui. Merci,* Monsieur."

And he shows her to a seat at the table. Duke is standing upright, but as she sits, he seems to fold into the chair next to her.

"Mademoiselle," says Jean-Luc.

"Please…call me Lilith," she says.

"Would you like me to put this cloak in my office for the moment?"

"Oh, yes, *merci.*"

Brigitte, the *bonne à tout faire,* brings forth a tray with coffee in a pot, a small pitcher of warm milk, a *baguette,* sweet Normandy butter, and a wedge of *gruyère.*

"Oh," exclaims Lilith, as Duke pours her coffee and milk together and hands the cup to her.

"That is so kind," she says, looking up into his face.

"My pleasure," he says with that beaming smile.

"Lilith," I say, from across the table. "What a lovely name," at which she nods, sipping her coffee.

"It is my mother's."

"Is your mother here with you in Paris?"

"Oh yes. We stay at the hotel next door...my mother, my aunts, and father. My brothers are home in Qatar. I am the only girl."

"You speak such good English, almost like a British person," I say.

"My school at home, it is run by British teachers. My father wants me to be educated in many things."

"You are lucky," I say, thinking of the number of articles I have read, dealing with education for women in Islamic countries, or lack of same.

"We are so glad you stopped by the Hotel Marcel. It is so nice to meet you," I continue.

"Yes," says Jean-Luc. "Please feel welcome here, any time."

Lilith blushes, smiles happily.

"Are you planning to go out?" I ask, wanting to add, without the burka, (but of course I don't.)

"I was hoping to go see The Eiffel Tower. I mean, I can see it from my balcony, but it's not the same as being, you know, right under it, at its feet."

"Of course," Duke says. "I can take you there. And have you yet been down to walk along the Seine?"

"No. I've crossed over it in the automobile, but it must be lovely to walk beside it."

At this moment, Sasha comes from behind the front desk, having just descended in the *ascenseur*.

"Hello, all of you."

We greet him in unison.

"Well, well. Who have we here?" he says, looking intently at Lilith. "What a beautiful addition to our little group."

"Her name is Lilith," Duke says somewhat defensively. "She's staying at The Majestic." Then he adds quickly, "I am taking her to The Eiffel Tower."

"Yes," Lilith quickly says. "I want to see Paris...really see Paris, not just through the window of a limousine."

"And Paris will surely love to see you," Sasha says, his tone serious.

"Listen," I interject, "if you're really going outside, it's very cold. I'd better lend you my coat. It's down-filled and quite warm. And some gloves." I leave the table, as she nods in agreement, and I go up to my room, descending with the brown coat and a pair of red cashmere mittens.

As I join the group at the table, I hear Lilith say, "They trail after me like I'm a piece of expensive jewelry to be stolen."

"If the bodyguards come back, what would you like me to tell them," Jean-Luc, says thoughtfully. "And they'll surely come back!"

"Hmm...I guess tell them I went to the Louvre *Musée*. Yes, My father would approve of that. He will be more angry at them—that I escaped them, than he will be with me." She gives a charming little laugh. "But please, oh please, do not tell them I shed my burka! That he could never forgive." And for a moment, Lilith looks scared.

"Of course," Jean-Luc says, reassuringly. "You'd best be off before those fellows come back looking for you."

On with my coat. On with my mittens. And Lilith, with Duke's hand beneath her elbow, starts toward the lobby door.

"*Un moment*," Jean-Luc says, stepping in front of them. He goes out on the stoop, looks in both directions, then beckons to the pair. "The coast is clear," he calls, and the two hurry past him, and go down the street in the opposite direction from The Eiffel Tower because if they went directly, they would have to cross in front of the entrance to The Majestic.

Jean-Luc watches them round the corner and aim for the Champ de Mars which will take them to the back-side of the tower. "*Bonne chance, young ones. Bonne chance.*"

"What a charming young woman," Sasha says to Jean-Luc, as they watch the retreating couple. "She has no idea that her face, that small-boned body, her height...she's tall for an Arab woman... but it's her expression—her 'innocence.'"

"Careful, Sasha, I know you!" warns Jean-Luc. Sasha burst out laughing. "Nah, Jean-Luc. It's just that she would make a great model."

"Hmmm," Jean-Luc muses. "I wonder what 'big-daddy,'" with a nod of his head toward The Majestic, "I just wonder what he would do if he should see his only daughter on the cover of *Vogue?*"

"Burn *Vogue* and The Majestic to the ground?" I say.

"Burn Sasha, more likely!" says Jean-Luc with an impish grin.

CHAPTER ELEVEN

En Face

BRIT. ME.

I have been avoiding him on the phone, hanging up abruptly the minute I hear his voice. He has called more than once. I decide I must speak with him the next time he rings. Sue's suggestion that I call him— well it's impossible. I just can't.

This has become ridiculous.

He phones again on Tuesday, evening about 6:00 o'clock.

"Yes," I say.

"Elizabeth." There is silence. "I've been trying and trying to reach you. What in God's name is the matter? You know we have waited…"

"You must know what's the matter, Brit. How could you not know?"

"I swear. I don't. For Christ's sake, tell me. You have never been reticent before."

"It's hard for me to mention her name."

"Whose name?"

"Marianna." My voice is low.

"What about Marianna?"

"She's back in your life? She didn't drown in the sea? No abortion. No miscarriage. No suicide. What a hideous fable you told me…"

"Just a minute," he interjects.

"No. I won't stop." The words keep coming. "I believed everything you told me, every little word and adjective and phrase."

"Stop, Elizabeth!"

"She's back. Living with you."

"Just stop! Please."

"She answered the phone when I called two days ago. When I asked who she was, she said 'Marianna.' What am I to think? Brit. What?"

"Now I get it. She didn't mention you called."

"Then I'm right. How can you do this, with all the sweet-talk you have poured over me."

"You're right and you're wrong," he says firmly. "The Marianna you spoke to—she is Marianna's mother."

I am stunned into silence.

"She showed up here in Paris about two weeks ago. We've always liked each other—a lot—she was happy that her daughter and I were together.

She was as distraught as I was at her death, and when I moved to Paris, we managed to keep in touch…oh, not a lot, but enough to maintain a friendship. Say something, Elizabeth. Say something."

Still, my silence.

"Elizabeth, I know you're there. I can hear you breathing."

"I'm here."

"Speak up. Please."

"Yes, I'm here," I say more loudly.

"Well?"

"I feel the fool."

For the first time, he laughs.

"Well, you have been a bit foolish. But I guess I can't blame you. How could you know?" He pauses. "She is here in Paris for a symposium. I asked her to stay with me. It's only for a couple of days."

"Oh Brit. I am sorry."

"No, darling. No. She never told me you called—that a woman had called. I can see why you might be shocked. Marianna! No wonder." He laughs. "But we have lost time. We have to make up for that."

I am so truly ashamed. I can't speak.

"Are you still there?" He waits a minute. "Would you like to meet her?"

"Yes," I breathe.

"Just to prove to yourself…"

"No," I interrupt. "Not for that. I'd like to meet her to know about her daughter, what she was like, and how she loved you." My voice is low, unsure.

"You want that?"

"Yes."

"Done and done," he says. "Tomorrow night? Do you want to come over to the Marais and the three of us can go to dinner over here?"

"Yes."

"Come to the house around 7:00." "I'll be there," I say. Brit hangs up, as I hear in my head the song, 'What Kind of Fool Am I?'

CHAPTER TWELVE

The Other Marianna

I ARRIVE AT #2 Bis, rue de Chance, in the Marais, Brit's small town house just before 7:00 PM Wednesday night. He answers my knock, strongly embraces me, and gives me a kiss to rock my world.

"Come in, sweetheart," he says in low tones. I see the familiar salon, rather dark, with a fireplace in the corner and a number of paintings leaning against the stone walls. I notice in one corner, an inflatable mattress, with blanket and pillow neatly placed on top.

"Marianna is upstairs in the studio. She's using my bed and bathroom while she's in Paris, probably for the next few days."

"I'll be right down," I hear a female voice call from above.

"Do you have the chance to paint if she's in your workroom with its easel and wide window?" I ask, but he does not answer because I see a small, blond woman in a flowered skirt, peasant blouse, and long beads, descend the wooden staircase and come forward to greet me.

"Hi," she says, her face and smile warm. She looks to be in her mid-70s, an aging hippy-like person, but truly attractive. I can't help but imagine Haight-Asbury as a part of her youth.

"Hi," I respond. As we shake hands, she turns to Brit and says, "My she is a pretty woman, Brit. You do well for yourself."

I laugh and say, "You're not bad yourself," and any reservations are broken.

"Anybody hungry?" he says, taking my hand. "It's not far, *La Cocotte*, and really good, if you like French comfort food," and we are out the door in the cold, evening light and make our way to a tiny *bistro* around the corner.

Inside it is nostalgic of the French countryside with bare wooden tables in honey-color, fawn-colored placemats and large white plates. There are metal candle stands on each table—of which there are only 12—and small pots of *fleur de lis*, soft, as centerpieces.

"They serve a fantastic *moules* with white wine and bread crumbs and herbs and a shot of cream…oh so good but pretty garlicky. If we all have it?" he says with a sidelong grin at me.

"Sounds mighty good to me," I say, as Marianna echoes my enthusiasm.

Brit orders a fine white *Pouilly Fumé*, and the mussels, but first we share a slice of *foie gras* with toasted pieces of *baguette*.

It is very intimate, this moment, for the three of us. I find Marianna extremely open, speaking freely of her daughter, of Brit's love for her, his grief, all this right in front of him, which does not seem to phase him in the least.

"She worked beside him, out in California. Small sculptures—wild animals, tigerines, wolves, fish, even. She was passionate about nature. She loved to swim." With this last remark, Marianna grows silent.

We all do, but the arrival of a steaming bowl of the *moules* shifts the mood miraculously. The aroma is rich with garlic and wine, and we proceed to devour the small mollusks, juices dripping, the mood lightening, and a general sense of wellbeing overcoming the three of us.

After a *crème brûlée*, with three spoons, we walk Marianna back to Brit's house, let her in, and in so doing, I invite her to have lunch with me the Saturday after Christmas, at *La Terrasse*.

"Just come to Hotel Marcel around noon," I say, "and we can walk over. They have great *quiches* and *omelettes au fromage*, and we can have a chance to talk about this one," giving a nod to indicate Brit.

"Careful, ladies," he says with a laugh that makes me know he is not displeased.

"I would love to lunch with you Saturday. It will be my final hurrah. I leave for Seattle Sunday morning."

"Agreed," I say, happy that I'll have the chance to learn more about Brit.

We walk down the hill to the avenue where we find a taxi stand. When he and I get into the cab, he gives the driver the address of my small hotel and then takes me in his arms. I know this will be a night to remember.

And so it turns out to be.

It is a long night of being locked together, rising and falling, laughing and weeping, wistful and euphoric. There are no adjectives to describe my sense of relief in his love, the sense of elation in his kiss, and the real joy of having Brit in my arms.

CHAPTER THIRTEEN

A Conspiracy

LILITH, ON HER fifth floor balcony of the royal suite at The Majestic, is next to Sasha's balcony on the fifth floor of Hotel Marcel. My photographer friend had moved there from a small room downstairs when the Japanese couple who had booked the room to the right of me, their vacation finished, left the hotel. He now shares the adjacent balcony with me on one side, and almost shares a royal suite Majestic balcony on the other, a suite which Lilith happens to occupy.

He has requested this move from Jean-Luc. "You know me. I can take pictures from anywhere—but the balcony is prime viewing." And, of course, Jean-Luc acquiesces.

So there is Sasha, and he has managed, in the course of a day, to get more than one photo of the glorious young Lilith. In one, she is standing in a pale caftan with a black velvet sash that outlines the slim waist and rounded bosom. She looks wistfully across the street to Duke's attic room. The top half of his door is open, and his face is there, looking equally wistful, gazing across to the balcony of the fifth floor of The Majestic. Their eyes are fixed, one on the other.

Because the balustrade of The Majestic balcony juts out several feet beyond that of the balconies at Hotel Marcel, the angle, with The Eiffel Tower behind her form, is spectacular.

There is another photograph of her in a sea-green silk bathrobe, her black hair loose, as she leans to look below at the tops of trees and the street. Again, the tower is a symbol in the rear, a symbol not only of Paris, but one of freedom.

It is Sasha's pursuit to have her booked for a real, modeling session. He knows that will be hard. He has already told Ray Guild of this project.

"It's her air of innocence that is so striking. And she's exquisite," he tells his friend at French *Vogue* over the telephone.

"Does she have any idea of your plans for her, dear heart?" Ray is full of caution.

"She doesn't even realize I've been taking her picture—at least not yet."

"What? After all, a young Arabic girl? I doubt it would ever occur to her, much less to her family!!! Pictures! Selfies! Can you imagine what 'father' would think of his virginal child appearing on the cover of a crass, superficial publication like *Vogue* ? You had better be prepared for those large bodyguards, Sasha! Put on your running shoes."

"Oh, don't be so negative, Ray. Wait 'til I show you what I'm talking about, why I'm so determined."

"Oh, all right. Let's meet for drinks at *La Terrasse*. That way there might be a chance I would actually see this creature, as she is staying nearby in the 'hood'."

"Tomorrow?" Sasha asks.

"Around 5:00."

"You realize it's Christmas Eve?"

"Yeah. Right. Thursday. I forgot. Well, I guess it's one way to celebrate. Anyway, bring the pictures." Ray rings off

CHAPTER FOURTEEN

Christmas Eve, Chez Croix

AS I STEP out onto my frosty balcony on Thursday morning, I see Sasha with camera in hand. It is about 10:00 on this Christmas Eve morning.

"Taking pictures already?" I say sleepily.

"Well, I have a marvelous object right next door. One never knows when she might appear and what her state of dress- or undress- will be."

"Oh, Sasha. You never change."

"No," he responds with a grin. "Actually, I have big plans for her." He tells me of his modeling project involving young Lilith and of his conversation with Ray. "I am to meet him tonight with a couple of photos I've already taken."

"I'd love to see them."

"Okay, I'll get them," and he disappears, returning with two.

"Wow!" I can't help myself. They are beautiful. She is beautiful. In the second one, the one in the green robe, tiny snow crystals had begun to fall that lend a magical air to the picture.

"These are truly wonderful, Sasha." In fact, I am awed.

"Can't you just see her on the cover of *Vogue?*"

"I can, but I'm not sure her 'big-daddy' could possibly accept this. I imagine he would be livid! He is notably strict, from what I understand," I say, "and that's putting it mildly."

"Maybe Lilith can get around him…you know, a precious daughter has a way with her old man, no?"

"I'm skeptical."

After several minutes, I return to my room. It is cold outside, and I see Sasha still remaining at his perch.

Tonight, I am to join Jean-Luc and Isabella for a Christmas Eve dinner at the Frontenac's. First, we are to have cocktails at the Croix' apartment, the one Jean-Luc is seeking to purchase, at 6:00. I am deeply curious to meet the mysterious Louise and her husband, Edouard Croix, she who Isabella describes as 'eccentric'. Hah! A new character or two in the mix.

And tomorrow! Ah tomorrow. Christmas! With Brit. All day. In the evening, we are to dine with Jean-Luc and Isabella at his apartment. Jean-Luc is 'preparing a Christmas feast,' he has told me, for the occasion.

I have been puzzling for days about a Christmas present for Brit. For his apartment? No. For his work? Impossible! From the heart? Absolutely.

Paints? A new easel? I wouldn't dare. He cares nothing for clothes, nothing whatever for jewelry, even nothing for a watch. (He's often late.)

There is only one thing I want from him, something I hope he will want from me too; to be together as much and as often as possible. So yesterday, I went to American Airlines and purchased a round trip, open-end ticket, Paris/NY/Paris, business class (not coach) to be used within a year. I then bought a black leather passport/ticket case, engraved in gold with the word 'Brit', which I picked up this afternoon.

I know he can well afford his own ticket, but when I give it to him tomorrow, we will be able to plan when we can be together again. I put the ticket in the case, no comment, no note. The present will speak for itself.

At 5:45, Jean-Luc calls from downstairs, I descend, and he, Isabella and I are ready to walk across to apartment building 2 to visit Edouard and Louise Croix for a drink. I have been to their fifth floor duplex before, first when rented by Sasha, and a second time when it was leased to Jillian Spenser, with young daughter, Amelia. Poor Jillian is now in a French jail, for art fraud, and lonely little Amelia, in England with her father.

As we leave the stoop of the Hotel Marcel, René Poignal suddenly appears from around the corner, hailing us as he approaches. As usual, the resolute detective wears his trench coat tightly belted *a l'Américain* (in his mind.)

"Madam Elizabeth," he calls. "Jean-Luc told me you were coming to Paris at Christmas time. Happy *Noël*," he exclaims to me, bowing to all of us.

"*Bon soir*, Monsieur detective," I say cordially. "*Et à vous, joyeux Noël.* When you come by again, I would like so much to catch up on Jillian and Kurt…"

"Indeed, Madame. There's not much to tell. Both are still in stir, 'heh heh', as they say in America—Kurt for a long time. He did commit murder. With the Spenser woman—Jillian—at least there were no bodies!" Another 'heh heh.'

"We have an appointment, René," Jean-Luc interjects.

"Of course—on your way—have a good night," and René tips his hand to his head in farewell. "*Et*, Madame Elizabeth—little lady *inspecteur—prenez garde*. Be careful. With you around, drama always seems to happen."

"Perhaps not this time," I say with a laugh.

When we enter the Croix apartment, the place has completely changed. Now occupied by the actual owners, the Croix couple, it is furnished in sophisticated detail, with pictures of Africa—the desert—a great river—herds of goats—and dark green upholstery on chairs and sofa. The lighting from multi-colored table lamps is low, seductive. There is a smell of incense in the air.

As our host and hostess move towards us, I am struck by the contrast—Edouard's conventional appearance—and the florid, yet secretive appearance of his wife. She is dressed in a long black garment, (a perverse kind of burka?) and her dark hair is thick and fuzzy. She wears a purplish lip rouge. Her eyes are small and inquisitive, as she appraises me from head to toe. She exudes an aura of hostile examination that belies the words of greeting she speaks.

"Come see, Elizabeth," Jean-Luc says, drawing me to the window. *"L'Hôtel, la bas."* Across the pots of geraniums on the Croix balcony, he points to the small Hotel Marcel sign proudly.

I nod in approval. I also notice that from the window of the Croix apartment, Lilith's balcony at The Majestic is visible, in plain view.

Edouard and Louise present us with glasses of champagne, roasted nuts, Greek olives in a red glass bowl. There is a large green fern next to the entrance door, with bits of tinsel suspended on it, the only sign of the season. The conversation is stilted, and I am made uncomfortable by the constant gaze of Louise.

"You are from New York City?" she asks.

"Yes. Born and bred," is my reply.

"You like Paris?"

I smile. "How could I not?"

She smiles back with small pointed teeth, but the light in her eyes is harsh.

"You know our friend here, Jean-Luc, he wants to buy this place, this apartment."

I nod.

"What do you think?"

"Me? Well, it's not for me to say. If he wants to live here, that's up to him, and you, of course."

"No, but what do YOU think?"

"I guess it would be great. He can keep an eye on his property across the street..."

"Exactly," Louise says, interrupting.

Edouard has said little, except for small *politesses*. Louise has completely ignored Isabella, which I find rude, and without her curiosity about me, the conversation is so ordinary as to be a crashing bore.

CHAPTER FIFTEEN

Christmas Eve, Chez Frontenac

TAKING OUR LEAVE of the Croix *ménage*, with a final toast to the coming new year and a 'happy Christmas,' we move on to the Frontenac's apartment next door in building 3.

There, the music of the 50s French pop singer, Charles Trenet, greets us, as Henriette, the *femme de ménage*, in black dress and white apron, opens the door and ushers us in.

Duke is already there and is standing awaiting the three of us, as Elise and Pierre Frontenac meet us effusively, with "Come in. Merry Christmas. Please do come in."

Pierre Frontenac certainly reveals a lighter, more welcoming personality than ever I've seen. He is truly likeable and gracious. The presence of Duke has done something to him. To me, that is evident. And his wife, Elise, is relaxed and at ease.

After more champagne and a tray of *gougères*, delicate cheese puffs, we sit at the dining table over what Elise refers to as 'the regular Christmas Eve special dinner in France.' "Then it's on to midnight mass."

"Not for me, I'm afraid," says Duke. "I have to go to work."

"Of course," Elise responds amiably as Henriette places before her a huge tureen from which exudes the most delectable aroma, and at her place, a stack of bowls and a large ladle. Henriette also deposits two baskets of *baguettes, beurre, et encore bouteilles de champagne* at each end of the table.

As Elise ladles forth the fish stew, she speaks of its history as Henriette passes each of us a bowl.

"*Ma mère*...we had this fish stew every Christmas Eve when I grew up. It is a tradition, isn't it Pierre?"

"And a wonderful one," he responds.

"It certainly smells marvelous," Duke interposes.

"Well, it should," she continues... " It is made with shrimp and mussels and scallops and saffron and the broth with garlic and wine..."

"You're making me hungry," Isabella chimes in, and everybody laughs.

"You are supposed to dip your pieces of *baguette* into the broth," and we all do, slurping away, the soup dripping from fingers, all of us in a most intimate kind of communion.

"I can see why this is so traditional," I exclaim. "It is absolutely divine."

This heavenly course is followed by a crisp green salad and the ubiquitous cheese board, plus *encore de champagne*. The mood over Elise's antique table is delightfully warm, the talk easy and flowing.

Duke describes *Le Club* and the comradery of the musicians. "I m so happy there, playing bass and jazz violin. People really like the sound." Then, gazing at Pierre and Elise, he blurts out, "It's like I've come home, with the music, and with you both."

The room is silent. All one hears are people breathing.

Duke, my young African-American friend's story, has been so fraught with angst—finding the Frenchman, Pierre Frontenac who fathered him so long ago—his mother dead of diabetes back in Chicago.

Then suddenly, looking at his father and Elise, Duke blurts out, "I didn't mean that quite the way it sounds..."

"It sounds just right to me, Duke," says Pierre, and Elise, sitting next to Duke, pats his hand. I am touched and exceedingly proud to have taken part in this critical reunion. All seems at peace.

After poached pears in wine and *madeleines,* that famous Proustian cookie, we adjourn to the living room, where Charles Trenet is replaced by Louis Armstrong singing "What a Wonderful World," which we all agree is just about right.

As we cross the street, Duke says quietly to me, "Can she borrow your coat again?" "She's going with you tonight?" I whisper, surprised. "Yes. She should be at Hotel Marcel waiting right now."

And she is there. I get the coat and I save her burka in my room.

I finally fall asleep wondering just how in hell the lovers will really face the music, the cacophony next door in another royal suite of The Majestic Hotel when the truth is known, a loud, violent blast from 'big-daddy' himself.

Mon Dieu!

CHAPTER SIXTEEN

Christmas

BRIT HAS ASKED me to lunch at his house in the Marais. He explains it will be simple, but he wishes to have a whole day alone with me in his world. Marianna is with her symposium friends for the holiday, and we will have his house to ourselves.

It is a frosty Friday, this Christmas morning. The streets are quiet as I make my way to a taxi stand. I have to wait some time, for the drivers are all at home with Christmas food and cheerful spirits. Finally one appears and takes me off to meet my love.

I wear a red dress under the puffy, down coat so often borrowed by Lilith. It has her scent, a sweet, musky perfume. I carry my Christmas present for Brit in a small, red gift bag.

Arriving at #2 Bis, rue de Chance, I pause at the door.

Before I can knock, it opens and he sweeps me into the downstairs room of the small town house, takes me in his arms and whispers 'Merry Christmas'.

Upstairs, he has spread out on a low table, our luncheon of *paté de campagne, cornichons, céleri rémoulade* in a white bowl, a beautiful, runny piece of *Brie, baguettes, macarons,* and a bottle of *Merlot,* "a great year," he explains.

We sit on the floor on two cushions he has placed next to the table. He prepares a plate for me, then one for himself. "I decided I am no cook, so I hope this will suffice. Besides, I expect a grand dinner *chez* Jean-Luc."

"I'm sure we will have one. He is practically a *chef de cuisine supérieure.*

Raising his glass, Brit looks at me, "Merry Christmas, darling. I can't imagine a happier one." He sets down his glass. "Wait, I have something for you." As he starts to get up, I say, "Well, I have a present for you too," and from beside me, I hand him the little, red bag.

"For me?" he says with fake surprise.

"Who else?"

He pulls out the leather case, handles it, caresses it. "This is beautiful," he says, happy as a child. He opens the case, takes one long look at the business ticket, American Airlines, Paris/NYC/Paris, then throws back his head with a mighty laugh.

I'm startled.

He gets up, goes to a drawer near the narrow bed and pulls out an envelope tied with a red velvet ribbon. He walks slowly over to me and with a sweet, wide smile on his face, hands it to me.

I undo the red velvet bow, open the envelope; a round trip ticket Air France, NYC/Paris/NYC. First class!

I leap to my feet and he swings me around. "We shall meet again more than once…in our two favorite cities," and he kisses me.

"Happy New Year, Brit. It will be one, because there is no way we won't be together," and we spend the rest of the day doing what lovers do best. Being in love.

At Jean-Luc's apartment that evening, we find our host and hostess eager to see us, welcoming us with glasses of champagne. The salon, with its open kitchen, is filled with the most delicious aroma of roasting meat. There is mistletoe over the entrance door—which Brit and I honor—and a small pine tree in the corner hung with silvery Eiffel Towers, brightly colored figurines of saints and small animals, with a crystal star at the top. Soft music fills the air with the sounds of the season, haunting and sweet.

We sit at the table near the window over the avenue. It is embellished by a low centerpiece of red roses to match the red wine glasses. We are plied with first, smoked salmon with *crème fraîche,* then an herb-crusted rack of lamb with *pomme de terre purée,* followed by a simple salad. More champagne flows with the *mousse au chocolat.* Both Brit and I are hazy with the best kind of fatigue, every muscle stretched, and limp with pleasure.

It seems that Jean-Luc and Isabella may have spent a similar kind of afternoon, because both of them are as hazy as we. The evening ends early and happily in Jean-Luc's apartment salon, a place resplendent and shining with love.

"Merry Christmas, you two," Brit says, on departing. "Happy New Year, you two," is Jean-Luc's reply, and that it surely promises to be.

CHAPTER SEVENTEEN

Lunch at La Terrasse

MARIANNA APPEARS IN the lobby of Hotel Marcel promptly at noon, this beautiful, chilly December Saturday, the day after Christmas. I am waiting for her, and together we meander over to the bistro so close to Hotel Marcel, *La Terrasse* through quiet streets.

There are outdoor heaters to warm the patrons sitting, drinking their wine, smoking their *Gauloises* on the sidewalk terrace, but we go inside and are greeted with easy familiarity (I have eaten there a lot.)

Seated at one of the red velvet booths, over a carafe of *Pinot Noir*, we order, for me, the *omelette au gruyère*, for Marianna, a *quiche Lorraine*, both accompanied by green salad in a lemon *vinaigrette*.

"I know you and Brit...I know you are more than friends," she says hesitantly.

"We are," I reply. "But I know too that he cared very much for your daughter. He loved her, calls her his 'artist-mate.'"

"Yes, that they were." Marianna takes a sip of her wine. But she... my daughter, she was complex—given to depression, but talented, very talented. And Brit, he helped her through those down times. He was wonderful with her. Sometimes I wondered how."

"How what?" I ask.

"How he could be so patient. Most men aren't," she says, with a sardonic little grin.

I laugh. "That's for sure!"

"In her early 20s, Marianna had a boyfriend. I couldn't stand him. We were living in San Francisco (Haight-Asbury, I wondered?) He was a hunk, but insensitive. And she, she was a rebel, you know, my girl was. When I found out he hit her, more than once, well...you can imagine."

"God," I say.

"When she got pregnant, he was long gone."

Our dishes arrive. My cheese omelet is delectably creamy. Just as I take a bite, I see the American couple from the bar in the Majestic Hotel, enter the dining room. Jerry, the noisy one, spots me, as they pass our booth to sit at a nearby table. God, I hope he doesn't notice me, but, unfortunately, he does.

"Well," he says, pausing before us, with Madge in tow. "You gotta' be American! Am I right?"

I nod.

"Saw you over at The Maj bar, the other night. Are you staying there too? Pretty grand, isn't it?"

I shake my head. "No, I am at the hotel next door."

"You mean that dinky place right beside The Maj?" His wife chimes in, her southern accent thick as glue.

"You mean you're at that Hotel Marcel? Why, Nelson, the headman at The Maj desk says that's a 'hotel of convenience,' if you get my meaning," Jerry says, grinning lasciviously.

"You know," Madge says. "For a couple who are hot...who want to... you know...who want a bed for an hour or two."

"That's absurd," I sputter. "The Hotel Marcel is not 'un hôtel de convenance,'" I say in my best French.

My tone of disgust seems to quash the conversation, and looking down their respective noses, they move on, thank God. I can just imagine Jean-Luc's furious reaction to this assumption.

"What was that all about?" says Marianna.

"That was about 'ugly Americans,'" I say. "You know they exist for sure when you see those two." Then, taking a needed drink from my wine glass, I continue, "but tell me more about your girl, young Marianna."

"Where was I?"

"She was pregnant."

"Oh yes. And, of course she had an abortion. God, after that she was really depressed. Even medication didn't help, not at all."

"Poor thing," I say, genuinely moved.

"So a few years later...when she lost Brit's baby...the miscarriage...well it really put her over the deep end. She called me in despair. I didn't know what to do. She felt such a failure as a woman."

"But these things happen."

"That didn't seem to matter. She wanted his baby desperately and even though Brit hadn't wanted a child particularly, he was more than prepared to support both mother and their little kid, both emotionally and with money."

"Would they have married," I inquire gently. Somehow, the answer to that question seems important.

"I don't think either of them needed that little piece of paper. But she did want his baby...oh so much. She thought he was beyond talented and their child might have both their gifts."

We order a second carafe and *deux espressos*. I notice the American man and wife are rapidly devouring *steak frites*, barely speaking to each other.

Then, thoughtfully, Marianna begins, "That awful night, she probably had a lot of vodka. She must have wakened near dawn, most likely feeling hung over—and so depressed. She went out on the beach and just walked into the sea she loved so passionately. She adored swimming, you know. She always went way out, but this night she went out so far and never wanted to return to shore."

Marianna's eyes are glistening. Mine too.

After a moment, I say, "Brit told me she died of cancer."

"Yes, he told people that. He was trying to protect her, her reputation. She wouldn't want people to know she ended her own life." Marianna takes a long pull on her wine glass. "He was upset...really upset...so much so, he went and had a vasectomy. I guess he kind of blamed the baby for what happened to my daughter."

"And he fled to Paris," I say.

"Yep. And here he stays—for good, I think. It's probably for the best. He's happy here." Then she gives me a long look. "You make him happy, Elizabeth. I can see it, the way he looks at you."

"It's mutual," I say, heart lifting. "Is it okay with you?"

"What? That you guys are happy? Of course," Marianna says. "How do they say it here in France? *Bien sûr?*"

"*Bien sûr,* indeed," I say. "I'm glad you're okay with it. It means a lot," and with that, we call for the check and head out into the bright, cold sunlight arm-in-arm and say a final goodbye.

CHAPTER EIGHTEEN

Lazy Sunday

I SLEEP LATE, luxuriating among the pillows. I can see through the glass doors to the balcony that it is snowing. Sound is muffled. The light in the sky is muted. All is serene.

I call Sue. We speak on the phone some minutes. I tell her of the mutual two-way tickets Brit and I exchanged.

"*Formidable*," she exclaimed. "Well, you know what they say about great minds! What a happy holiday for the two of you."

We giggle together and make a date for lunch at *Caviar Kaspia* for next Wednesday.

"What's up for your New Year's Eve?" she asks.

"I've no idea."

With that, she hangs up and I rise to put myself together for a late breakfast downstairs.

As I enter the lobby, I see Jean-Luc sitting on the salon sofa with Louise Croix. It is about 11:00 o'clock. Jean-Luc is rarely at the hotel on week-ends, but because of the possible sale of the apartment across the street, I determine that is probably the reason for him being here on a Sunday.

The two are deep in conversation. They don't even say hello as I go to the far end of the salon table so as not to be intrusive. Brigitte brings me *café au lait* and the usual rolls and butter and cheese, which I eat slowly. I can hear his rumble of French and her low, sultry voice in response from the purple-rouged lips. The words are vehement, heated.

I drop my spoon by mistake causing a clatter, at which they both look toward me and for the first time, see me. I give a little embarrassed wave.

Now uncomfortable, the two decide to join me.

"Merry Christmas again," says Louise.

"And to you too," I reply. She is gazing at me intently which makes me even more clumsy.

"Where is the black boy? I see he comes here to breakfast with you many times," Louise says.

"Who?" I say, furious.

"You know, the one who lives in my attic."

"You mean Duke Pierre Davis, the African-American musician?" I say through clenched teeth.

"He's the one."

"He's obviously not here for breakfast today."

"True...but he comes often, no?"

I do not reply.

"He has his eyes on that Arab girl at The Majestic. And I see her, on her balcony, gazing back."

"What do you mean?" I am appalled that this nasty woman has noticed. Poor Duke and Lilith. They have been that obvious and it is dangerous.

"She's nothing to mess with. He'd better watch his step," Louise comments as she walks away. It sounds like a threat.

"Or?" I call after her.

She just turns and gives an insipid little smile over her shoulder.

I decide I have to get out of here. I grab an umbrella from a stand in the lobby, put on the brown coat, and decide to walk in the gentle snowfall to clear my head and ears of that woman's voice.

I leave the building and cross the street. I stand next to building 2, where the Croix couple live, with Duke above in their attic room, 'the black boy,' she had called him. I look across at the fifth floor of The Majestic to Lilith's balcony. She is not there.

I look up to the sixth floor of building 2. I really cannot make out Duke's attic door, but I can tell from the angle, he has a perfect view of Lilith, as she does of him. Louise's awareness of their lonely, visual contact is nerve wracking because she is an unpredictable, unpleasant woman who could do ill to those of whom she is jealous.

I turn up the street toward the Champ de Mars.

It is snowing harder. As I pass building 1, head down under the umbrella, I almost trip over the Shih Tzu, Schnitzel, on his red leash. I look up into the face of Dr. Guillaume Paxière.

He looks at me astonished. "Elizabeth?"

"Yes. I'm afraid it's me."

"Guillaume." I hear the angry voice of Sylvie LaGrange. She is standing next to the doctor, looking unduly sour at the sight of me. "You know her?" she asks him.

"We have met," he says formally. To me, he says, "You are staying at The Majestic?"

"No, no," I sputter. "At the Hotel Marcel…always at the Hotel Marcel."

"Of course."

"We can't stand here in this," Sylvie complains. Schnitzel is making a yellow line in the snow. "Come along, Doctor," she says, tugging at his sleeve. She has yet to say hello to me, although she knows full well who I am.

I take a long look at her. She is thinner, but bulky in her *faux* fur fox coat, an orange color that does not become the red hair. She wears heavy makeup and has on expensive leather boots.

As she pulls him away and drags the dog through the snow, Dr. Paxière tips his hat to me and says in low tones, "I'll be in touch," which

Sylvie happens to hear. Her face red with anger, she really pulls the poor man toward the cross street leading away, gesticulating angrily at him, shaking her finger in his face. I doubt this goes well with him.

Oh God! I 'll have to cope with him at some point, I expect, although maybe she will intimidate him sufficiently that he will forget.

Such nasty people! Thankfully, there are the others, like my Brit, my Sue, Jean-Luc and his Isabella, and Duke and his Lilith, and Sasha and Ray. The snow is lessening and as the flakes drift down, my happier thoughts, like birds, fly up to meet the glistening crystals before they melt.

CHAPTER NINETEEN

Monday, Day 10

WE ARE BREAKFASTING, Duke and I, on this Monday, the 10th day of my Paris visit. As Louise Croix noticed, we have taken to sharing our *café au lait* and crispy *croissants* on frequent mornings on my sojourn. He has become a true pal of mine and an enthusiast as passionate as I about Paris.

And passionate about something else.

"I took Lilith to *Le Club* on Christmas Eve after the Frontenac dinner."

"I know, Duke, remember? I kept her burka in my room. Antoine let you in about midnight to retrieve it, don't you remember?"

"I forgot," he says, flushing.

"Yes, but I remember for sure…having to get up at that hour," I say with a teasing grin. Duke looks sheepish. "But, tell me. How did she like the music—and your part in it?"

He flushes again. "She said she was 'enchanted.'"

"That's quite a word, Duke…enchanted."

"I know. She said she isn't allowed to hear such music." Proudly, he continues, "She particularly loved my violin solo, said she'd never imagined that instrument could be so modern." Duke laughs. "She is really beginning to get rid of what she calls 'her burka mentality.' Can you imagine?"

I laugh. "Rid of that horrible, confining, cumbersome piece of cloth! What a lock on her nature it must be."

"She told me she stays docile before her father and mother and 'aunts.' They are not really aunts—they're more like extra—I don't know—women for her father. Somehow, Lilith accepts that. Underneath that heavy cloth she is forced to wear and a passive smile—well beneath all that…"

"There is a tenacious young woman."

"That she is! Exactly She's determined to see the world, be of the world." Duke's face is radiant when he speaks of her. "I gave her a little present…you know, for Christmas. It's a thin gold chain she can wear around her neck."

"The better to hide it," I say, thinking of the heavy burka.

"I had a charm attached. A gold charm, a little gold key."

"Key?"

"Yes. A key to the future, a key to life."

"A life…with you?" I say. He nods. "Oh Duke, you'd best be very careful."

"Of what?"

"Of what you dream of."

With that, Jean-Luc comes towards us from the back office. I beckon him to join us.

"How's it going with the lovely Lilith?" he asks Duke, with a twinkle.

The young man just grins.

"I take it all is going great, from that big smile."

Duke only smiles harder. Then he asks Jean-Luc, "Have those bodyguards been around?"

"No. They haven't, thank God. They think we are too poor a hotel for a girl like Lilith to take refuge in."

"You can say that again," I interject. "I have been meaning to tell you what those awful Americans told me when I had lunch at *La Terrasse* on Saturday."

Jean-Luc's expression is quizzical, eyebrows raised. "What? What'd they say?"

"They told me that the supercilious manager at The Maj...Nelson...I think that's his name... insinuated that the Hotel Marcel is a tawdry establishment, '*un hôtel de convenance*,' a...you know...where..."

"I know what it means!" Jean-Luc splutters, his face turning red. "This I do not forget!" he says angrily, getting to his feet.

On leaving the table to go up to my room, I pass Jean-Luc at the lobby desk. I am struck by the fury of his expression. His face is cold and compressed with rage, and he seems to be muttering to himself.

Perhaps I should have left unsaid the remarks of Jerry and Madge, but in all truth, I could not keep silent. I was as outraged as Jean-Luc, well, maybe not <u>that</u> furious, but close.

In the *ascenseur*, I think of Duke. He has fallen in love with the impossible. I hope he can treat this romance with a modicum of restraint and reality.

That's foolish, I think. How can a young man of 20 control the soaring feelings that accompany first love, nor a girl, kept in wraps, literally, for her whole life, contain herself when she finds an eager accomplice to show her a rosy world through loving eyes?

Romeo? Juliet? The balcony? Good Lord. They have nothing compared to Duke and Lilith. Yet, it's the same old story, now isn't it!

CHAPTER TWENTY

The Persuaders

AS I COME into the breakfast salon, this Tuesday morning, I see Sasha and Ray Guild, deep in conversation over their coffee cups, crumbles of baguette on plates before them.

"Hello, you two," I say gaily. "Pretty early for the likes of you, no?"

"Hah," says Ray. "We are colluding."

"Is that a word?" I respond.

"In this case, it is. We want to get the little Lilith to pose for Sasha's camera at The Eiffel Tower," Ray continues.

"Her delicacy, next to the harsh metal structure of the leg of the tower will be spectacular," Sasha remarks. "I can't wait for such a picture. We've got to persuade her. And you...you can help."

"Uh, uh," I say, shaking my head 'no'—"not a chance. You realize, fellows, she has an extremely autocratic father and several body guards who at this point have no idea she has been running around Paris burka-less. They would be appalled. And I'm sure they can be really mean."

"Tough," says Ray sarcastically.

"Tough? You've got to be kidding. You know what can happen to a young Arab woman. And what do you want her to wear, a bikini?"

"Of course not," says Sasha. "Nor a burka. Maybe that pale green robe…"

At this moment, Duke appears from his attic room across the street. He wears a big grin.

"Hey," I say to him. "Come hear and listen to these two. They have plans for Lilith."

Duke sits next to Ray. "What plans?" Duke is concerned.

"I want her for the cover of *Vogue*."

"You gotta' be kidding! No way."

"Why not, Duke? You could help us persuade her. She really likes you."

"Impossible," the young man says, squirming in his chair.

"If anyone can convince her, it would be you," say Ray persuasively.

"Listen. She's in enough danger going around with me, much less being on public display…"

"Look. She's got to be 18. She has to have some rights." Sasha is adamant.

"Rights," Duke exclaims. "What rights? You guys are crazy if you think a young girl from a country such as Qatar can do anything she wants…be out in the world like an American. Forget it."

"But this is France, not Qatar. She might have protection here," exclaims Ray.

"But not there—in her home country. The repercussions might be terrible," I say, genuinely upset by the thought.

"Nothing bad's going to happen, you two," says Ray. "Listen, I'm determined…She's just too good a subject…too exciting…hey, and maybe we should leave it up to her?" he says suddenly smiling.

We all turn to see Lilith in her burka enter the lobby. She is breathless, eyes flashing. She rushes over to stand by Duke who has risen. He takes her hand. "Don't listen to these guys," he says in warning.

"Why?" is her response.

"Because…"

But Sasha interrupts Duke. "Mademoiselle," he says in his most dulcet voice, "I, as a photographer, want more than anything to take a real portrait of you. You are really beautiful," he says, and one can see a hint of a blush on her lovely face. She lowers her lashes.

"I am not trying to flatter you or embarrass you," Sasha goes on. "But you are a classic beauty…"

"Just stop this," Duke says, angrily.

"No, Duke. It's all right." As there is no one but us in the lobby, Lilith begins to wriggle out of the heavy cloth. I wonder if she is not becoming a bit careless.

Wearing a sky blue dress to the floor, shaking her dark hair free from the chador, she is a lithe, youthful creature, a brilliant vision.

"What a model she can be," mutters Ray under his breath.

"Come now," Sasha says, his voice eager. "Just as you are. The dress is perfect on you. It's a gorgeous sunny day, and The Eiffel Tower will make a backdrop that cannot be surpassed." Then turning to me, he says, "Can we borrow your coat?"

I had slung my down coat, with the red mittens in the pocket, over the back of an adjoining chair.

"I don't know." I am hesitant.

"Now, just a minute," Duke says, anxious.

"I want to do it, Duke," Lilith says, turning to him, looking up into his eyes. He finds her irresistible, but then, who wouldn't?

"Oh, here," I say, grabbing my coat and handing it to her. "Go ahead. I guess you can't get into any more trouble than you're already in."

Have I made a great mistake?

The three men surround the down-clad figure. They leave the hotel and go in the opposite direction from The Eiffel Tower to avoid passing The Majestic.

And just in time. As I go back to the *ascenseur* to squeeze myself into the box-like space, I see René Poignal on the stoop of the Hotel Marcel. He is watching the retreating backs of the three men and the small, down-coated figure they protect. He scratches his head, standing there, curious, until the little group is lost to view.

He comes into the lobby, notices me, gives a little wave and a smile, which I return. Trembling, I enter the elevator and rise to my fifth floor room, burka in hand and a fearful alarm in my heart.

CHAPTER TWENTY-ONE

Oh Careless Love

I THROW LILITH'S burka on my bed. I find the garment repugnant, its texture, the dark color, but most important, what it represents. I sit looking at it, thinking of that lovely young woman drowned in its folds. Will she have to resume wearing it? It would seem she will have to wear it again, at some dreadful moment in the future. How can she escape?

The phone rings.

"Elizabeth," a male voice says, in unctuous tones. "It's Guillaume."

I say nothing.

"You are there I know. You picked up the receiver."

"Yes?"

"I'm calling to see if we might lunch."

"Out of the question," I say abruptly. "Besides, I doubt that the widow LaGrange would appreciate our meeting."

"She does not own me, Elizabeth."

"Not yet," I hang up.

How dare he!

I go to the balcony with my binoculars at the ready. I look across at the LaGrange apartment. The blinds are drawn, although it is a bright day full of sunshine. In the salon of the Croix apartment in building 2, at the window, which is filled with light, I see the figure of Edouard looking upward towards the fifth floor balcony of The Majestic. He stands there, peering eagerly, seeming to seek to see who might be there. I notice Louise approach from behind him. I observe her pull his arm, turning him away from the window and with a quick movement, kick him hard in the leg. I see him wince, then walk away from her with a slight limp.

Nice lady, that Louise.

Sue and I have arranged to enjoy a pre-New Year's lunch at our haunt, *Caviar Kaspia*, this Tuesday. In my room, I put on a bright red jacket over a black turtleneck sweater. My coat is obviously elsewhere, somewhere near The Eiffel Tower (probably on the ground,) but my jacket is of heavy wool, and, the sun, midday, is at its highest warmth, so I feel prepared to face the Paris street.

Caviar Kaspia is dressed for the holiday with tall green boughs in vases, the scent of pine in the air, and a sprig of mistletoe on each table. The well-dressed crowd emits a festive glow in the upstairs dining room with its soft lighting and muted décor.

Sue awaits me on a banquette near the window. She carries a small package in her hand, which she gives me with a little bow.

"Merry Christmas. Happy New Year. Come back to Paris because I already miss you," she says, leaning forward with a kiss on my cheek.

"Oh, Sue. I have nothing…"

"You don't need to. I have you for the moment and that's enough for me. Go ahead. Open it."

I tear away the tissue and find a small black velvet bag. Inside is the tiniest rectangular box in pure gold.

"You see, you slide the top of the box and underneath, a lady can carry her pills."

I burst out laughing.

"It's quaint, isn't it," Sue says, laughing with me. "It was my mother-in-law's—she died, you know. Anyway, a French lady—and probably any real lady—would carry this in her evening purse."

"For her pills?"

"What else?"

"It's adorable," I say, and the two of us settle down to the usual gossipy interchange.

I am bursting with worry about Lilith, which I impart to Sue. I tell her of the possible *Vogue* picture and the insistence of Ray Guild and Sasha. I speak of Duke's devotion, when she interrupts with the remark, "Just how do you think that will go down with the emir?"

"Exactly! I'm worried sick."

"You know, this is getting to be no joke," Sue says, cutting a small piece of smoked salmon and placing it on buttered toast. She squeezes a lemon wedge over the pink fish, places three capers on top, and devours it.

"I know. I have no idea how her father will react. It may not be so bad. She has told me he is interested in her education."

"Well, that's rare in itself, isn't it? But this photo…it has nothing to do with 'education,' now does it?"

"A picture on the cover of a women's magazine devoted to fashion… and a romance with an African-American jazz musician…well, that's a lot for…"

"Real deal-breakers." Sue continues with her salmon. I do too.

"You know," she says, "we have no idea what we're talking about because we have no idea who we're dealing with, what this Emir is capable of."

I continue, between sips of ice-cold vodka, to report the adventures on the street of Hotel Marcel. I speak of Dr. Guillaume Paxière and Sylvie LaGrange. I tell Sue of Monsieur Marcel's desire to buy the apartment across the street from Edouard and Louise Croix, and what an unpleasant woman she is.

"I never knew a little hotel like Hotel Marcel could be so exciting. I envy you. In Montoire…in my château… no such dramas exist. It's quite boring. But I must say, it suits me anyway."

"Well, you're not boring. That's for sure."

"I should hope not," she says with a grin.

I return to the 'exciting' small hotel, replete and happy, to find the foursome of earlier in the day in the lobby, chatting with Jean-Luc about their Eiffel Tower photo shoot. Sasha and Ray talk excitedly. Lilith, divested of my coat, is radiant in her blue dress, and Duke beams down on her like the sun itself.

"Hey," I say, looking around. "Aren't we all being a little careless?"

"Probably," says Jean-Luc. "There's no one else here now...but..."

I grab Lilith's hand and bring her back to the stairs. "Climb up to the fifth floor. I'm coming up in the elevator and we'll get that burka back on you."

Mission accomplished.

Returning with her to the lobby where the three conspirators and Jean-Luc are sitting at the salon table. Lilith in her burka, and I join them.

Evidently, it has been decided that this evening, we are all to go to *Le Club* to celebrate the photo and pre-New Years.

"Are you crazy?" I exclaim.

"No," says Duke. "We are so happy." He comes over to me and gives me a hug. "Don't spoil it, Elizabeth. It's once in a lifetime."

CHAPTER TWENTY-TWO

Once in a Lifetime

"IT ONLY HAPPENS when I dance with you." That's what the band is playing this Tuesday night at *Le Club* as one of their musician members—the bass player—dances with an olive skinned girl in a pale blue dress. The band members all adore Duke. And why not? A more genuine, sweet tempered young man is hard to find.

Duke has taken this short break to be able to hold Lilith in his arms and to sway with her to the music. They are tight together on the small dance floor. People watch them because they are beautiful and so obviously in love that it is a joy to behold.

I sit with Brit at my side, his hand held in mine. We watch Duke and Lilith, then turn to each other with a similar smile, as if to say, 'we know what they feel.'

The song ends. Duke holds her for several extra beats, then jumps up on the stage and goes to his bass, which is leaning against the back wall. His face is suffused with happiness. For him, it has been some day, with anxiety over the photo session at The Eiffel Tower, the glorious result yet to be developed of the photograph of Lilith, and now, the bliss of holding her to him in a tight embrace, her body soft and yielding against him.

When the band stops for its regular 15-minute break, Duke comes to join Lilith, Sasha, Ray, Brit and myself at the table.

"Only champagne for tonight," Sasha has decided in advance. There are already two empty bottles on the table, but the waiter brings a third and our flutes are filled, our senses sated. We laugh together. Lilith and Duke are silent, hands touching on the table before them. They toast one another before he returns to the stage as she reluctantly lets him go.

"It's getting late," Ray says, not bothering to hide a yawn. "You kiddies can stay, but I for one am ready to call it a day. And what a day!" He has risen to his feet.

Lilith's eyes have not left the stage and Duke's face.

"I think it's best," I say gently to her. She nods, a dutiful 'yes.' Then she emits a deep sigh.

Sasha says to her, "We'll see you to Hotel Marcel…to get the burka. I can take you to the door of The Majestic." With that, as Brit pays the tab, we get up as one and aim for the exit.

Before we reach the bottom of the stairs leading up to the street, Lilith breaks away, runs toward the stage, and stands at the edge. Although in the midst of the soul song, "Georgia on my Mind," Duke sets his bass aside, runs toward her, leans down, and kisses her on the lips, at which the audience breaks into applause.

Oh my God, I think. What would the emir say? It's beyond imagining. The once in a lifetime day is over. We manage to get to Hotel Marcel in one piece, me clutching myself against the cold in my red jacket (and Brit's arm around me,) and Lilith in my brown coat and red mittens.

At the hotel, in my room, Lilith is burka-rized once more and with Sasha as escort, is able apparently to slip into the sleepy La Majestic hotel without notice.

Whew! Once in a lifetime. Right!

CHAPTER TWENTY-THREE

The Picture

I SLEEP LATE, this Wednesday morning. On awakening, I lie in bed, going over in my mind every detail of last night. Lilith and Duke are so obviously crazy for each other. Their situation is so full with danger. There seems to be no way they can ever be together. I worry for him, but my concern for her is palpable.

It is too late for breakfast, so I dress and make my way down the adjacent avenue (I have my coat, thank goodness, the day is frosty,) to a little restaurant with only eight tables. It is run by an older couple. The name of the tea-room-like dining place? *Pain et Chocolat.*

I order a sandwich of *jambon et beurre,* on a *baguette,* with a *café noir,* and just as I raise the cup to my lips, Dr. Guillaume Paxière enters the small establishment. He promptly sits down at my table with an obsequious smile.

"I didn't invite you," I say, after a long look.

"I know."

"Did you follow me here?"

"As a matter of fact, I did."

"And why, may I ask?"

"Ah, Elizabeth. I did not like the way we ended."

"In the first place, there is no 'we,'" I say angrily. "Besides, my God, it was five years ago."

"Time makes no difference."

"Please, doctor. Please leave me alone."

"I cannot. I do not like to be rejected," he says with a sardonic smile. "I am not used to that. Most women feel lucky…"

"Not this woman," I interject, and suddenly, I see an irate Sylvie LaGrange storm through the door of the restaurant, move beside Guillaume Paxière and box him on the ear.

"*Bâtard!*" she shrieks. Sylvie then turns to glare at me with such hatred, it almost glistens in the air.

The six or so customers look up from their lunches curiously, but without alarm. In Paris, perhaps this kind of lover's confrontation happens often.

Who knows?

The poor doctor rises. His demeanor is one of humiliation. "You have followed me, Sylvie," he says with disgust. (I find the remark ironic in view of the fact he has been doing the same to me.) She does not respond.

Guillaume Paxière bows slightly to me, says, "*Excusez moi et pardon,*" and exits with Sylvie LaGrange leading the angry way.

Good riddance to them both, I think. Recovering from this confrontation, I realize I am privately amused and proceed to enjoy my sandwich and coffee immensely, even though the restaurant customers have begun to glance slyly at me, or avoid looking at me altogether.

On my return to the hotel, I see Sasha, Ray, and Jean-Luc poring over a document at the far end of the salon table near the kitchenette door. They are hovered over the paper and speak in hushed tones, Ray gesticulating with his hand in wide gestures.

As I approach, I hear him say, "We can airbrush in a crumpled burka in the snow," to which Jean-Luc remarks, "Don't you think that makes it too political?" at which I say, "What's too political, her burka?"

The three turn to me. "Oh, it's you Elizabeth. Come look," says Ray. "This is sensational!" and he presents me with a glossy sheet of paper with a number of small, similar pictures of Lilith at The Eiffel Tower, and a second piece with a full-blown shot of the individual picture Ray has chosen.

The latter is extraordinary. One dark lock of Lilith's hair is entwined in a wrought iron curlicue on one of the base pillars to the tower, (one of its four feet, in reality.) With red mittens, she clutches the cold metal structure, as if attempting to climb to the top. With upturned nose, her expression vivid, she yearns to be free. It is the face of one who wishes to be unfettered. Underneath, in the shadow of her eyes, there is fear.

The pale blue dress, the color of Paris skies, clings to her stretched body as she reaches upward. At the bottom of the photograph, her bare toes touch a patch of snow. There is something rapturous in the picture because the girl seems to be clinging to a dream. Emotive enough to make one cry, Lilith presents a stunning image.

I am breathless. "My God," I finally say.

"Isn't she something?" Sasha gushes.

"What a cover!" Ray is burbling with excitement.

"Oh, Ray. You can't!" I am overcome with nameless fear.

"What do you mean I can't? Of course I can. And I will!" Ray sounds angry, which is indeed rare for him.

"But think of Lilith," I say. "Can you imagine the trouble she'd be in if this ever saw the light of day?" I am shaking the photograph under Ray's nose.

"Don't you think it's up to Lilith?" he says.

"No. I don't. I think it's up to Hamad al-Boudi." I am shouting.

"Who the hell is that?"

"Her father, Ray. Her father!"

We all sit down, take separate chairs, deflated, disappointed, and dismayed.

I know it should not happen, this picture on the cover of *Vogue*. Her father! Without his approval, Lilith cannot move. Without his consent, Lilith cannot appear. But most important of all, aside from the cover photo, without Hamad al-Boudi's acceptance of Duke, the young love affair is doomed.

Deep in thought, I hear Jean-Luc say softly, "Uh oh." He quickly begins to collect the glossies and put all in the accompanying manila folder, just as René Poignal approaches.

"*Allo, allo,* one and all," René says, greeting us with a smile. "Why such glum faces? I am here to wish each of you a *Bonne Année.* Cheer up, *mes amis.*" He takes a good look around and says, "What's the worry? Why are all of you so...*morose?*"

"Just tired," I say, as Jean-Luc rushes to the kitchenette, retrieves a bottle of good red wine, and returns with glasses and an opener.

"*Bonne Année,*" he says gaily, as he proceeds to decant the lovely liquor into glasses for each of us. "A toast to the New Year," Jean-Luc says, addressing me in particular. "I am so glad to have you here with us at this season, Elizabeth."

"My pleasure," I say with a grin, raising my glass to each in the room.

"*Eh,* Madame Elizabeth. What's up with you? With your binoculars, have you picked up any new troubles from the balcony?" René says, his head cocked suspiciously.

I smile sheepishly. If René knew of my hiding a burka, of lending my little Arabic friend, Lilith, my coat to disguise her, of helping Duke transport her to a jazz club, of their Romeo/Juliet romance, of a father-in-waiting, ready to blow sky high, and the girl clinging to The Eiffel Tower? Well, I can only guess his degree of disapproval, to put it mildly!

"Why nothing, Monsieur detective," I say. "Nothing seems to be happening at all." I run over to him and boldly kiss him lightly on each cheek. "*Bonne Année,* inspecteur. *Bonne Année.*"

René Poignal looks startled at first, but then responds with a smile and a bow. "And to you too, Madame Elizabeth, *ma petite inspectrice, Bonne Année à vous.*"

CHAPTER TWENTY-FOUR

New Year's Eve

I AM SPENDING the night at Brit's. We plan a private dinner at *La Cocotte*, just the two of us. Time is running out for my visit. Oh, yes, there is another week or so, but each minute seems precious as the day of departure approaches.

I arrive early at his house in the Marais. There is a bottle of champagne in an ice bucket on the table in the center of the salon on the first floor. On it, I see a small, black velvet box. A fire is glowing in the grate of the fireplace. Brit's delight in greeting me feels like a warm robe about my body, so cold from the frosty night outside.

We say little. He pours the wine. We sit in the two easy chairs in the room before the fire. He rises, goes to the table, and brings to me the black box.

"Happy New Year," he says, kneeling down beside me and handing me what is in his hand. I open it. Within I see, nestled against a white satin cushion, a pair of diamond studs.

"Oh, Brit." I can hardly breathe. They are gleaming, catching the light from the fire and emitting their own small flames. "So beautiful. I don't know what to say."

"Nothing's necessary. I bought them for you because they remind me of our first night together in your room at the Hotel Marcel, where The Eiffel Tower lights filtered through the raindrops, sparkling our bodies with diamonds. It was the first time we made love."

"How well I remember, and the glorious picture you made about that night, 'Diamants en Pluie.' It is such a splendid picture, the hit of your show last May," I say, leaning forward to kiss him.

"I love you, Elizabeth."

"It's mutual darling." I never dreamed that at this ripe age of mine I could possibly hear the music of love and feel the passion of youth. How grateful, how happy I am.

At *La Cocotte*, we sit close to another hearth, my diamond studs, now on my ears, catching the firelight. The place is not crowded. It is a humble venue, but there is the sound of soft melody in the air, and the *service* is impeccable.

After starting with *coquilles St. Jacques*, Brit and I share a perfectly roasted *poulet aux morels*, more champagne, and finally a glazed apple tart with *crème fraîche*.

"The apple tart is always meant for good luck in France," he announced happily.

"Nobody's ever been as lucky as I," I exclaim. "Maybe it's the apple tart."

"Of maybe it's me," he says with a delicious smile.

We plan to go to *Le Club* to hear Duke and his band and celebrate the New Year, but instead, we walk slowly arm-in-arm down the cobbled street to Brit's town house. I find the little bed on the second floor ample for two and the music of love entrancingly beautiful.

I wear my diamond studs. I think I will never remove them. They are part of me.

And so is he.

CHAPTER TWENTY-FIVE

Happy New Year, One and All

IT IS NEW Year's Day. A Friday. I do not know where the day goes. We spend time wandering *La Place des Vosges*, the *parc* itself with its old-time gas street lamps and the arcade with small art galleries and jewelry shops and clothing stores. A street band plays gay music near a bistro with outdoor seating beneath the arcade roof.

Brit and I enjoy *soupe à l'oignon*, under its crust of melted cheese. It warms the heart on this frosty afternoon. Since we first met, since we have been separated so often by the Atlantic Ocean, we have written each other, not emails, but letters. Real letters. Love letters. I tell him how I keep his words on paper in a special leather box.

He tells me he keeps mine in the drawer at the base of his easel, "my most cherished space."

What can I say? We are in love.

He drives me back to Hotel Marcel around five in the afternoon in the Peugeot. We are silent on the ride. We enter the lobby together to find Jean-Luc behind his check-in desk with René Poignal in trench coat, leaning on the outer edge.

"Again, another *Bonne Année, inspecteur?*" I say, a query which he responds to with "Not exactly." His tone is serious. He looks like a man with a rather unhappy task to perform.

On the couch in the lounge area near the salon, I see Louise and Edouard Croix sitting stiffly, her feet crossed one over the other. She appears triumphantly sour and stares at me in her usual unnerving fashion.

"Is something wrong?" Brit asks René.

"We are waiting for someone," is the policeman's non-committal response.

I am suddenly cold. "Who?"

René does not answer. I notice Jean-Luc's face is lined with worry. Nobody says anything.

Several minutes go by when two men enter the hotel each one in a black suit, one carrying a kind of wood baton. I realize that they are two of the Emir's bodyguards.

"Messieurs." René greets them. "You have something to report to me?" he asks the larger of the two, the one with the baton.

"I am glad you speak English, sir." The man nods. "I do not speak French. And yes, we want to tell the police that this hotel," he says, eying Jean-Luc sitting at his desk, "this hotel has been providing a refuge for the daughter...the only daughter, I might add...of Hamad al-Boudi, who stays at The Majestic," again looking at Jean-Luc disdainfully.

"What do you mean 'providing a refuge', Monsieur?" René asks.

"The daughter comes here. She has been seen by the two people over there on the couch—who reported it to me this morning –she has been seen coming to this establishment, leaving her burka—somewhere HERE!" he says loudly, "and going about the Paris streets in an old brown coat, wearing red mittens."

"What is your name, sir?" René asks the man, to interrupt his tirade and diffuse the situation.

"Ahmed," is the reply. "Hamad al-Boudi does not permit his daughter to run free like this in western attire and without my escorting her. She is a child…"

"She's over 18 years old," I interject.

"And just who are you?" Ahmed says to me menacingly.

"Just a minute," René says. "Ahmed, in the first place, it is not illegal in France to go about in western clothes. It is not illegal for her to come to this hotel for a few minutes. It is not illegal for a girl of 18 to move about Paris unescorted. So what do you and Mr. Boudi…"

"Hamad al-Boudi, please," Ahmed says, half-insulted. "He wishes this behavior stopped by the police."

"You can tell him that there has been no French law broken here in Paris. We are not in Qatar, after all, where such behavior may be treated differently."

"We are certainly not in Qatar!" Ahmed shouts in frustration. "What am I to tell Hamad al-Boudi? That the police can do nothing?"

Yes," says René. "You go tell him that."

The two turn on their heels and leave the Hotel Marcel rapidly.

Jean-Luc, still sitting behind the check-in desk, is aghast. Brit and I start to laugh. René is shaking his head in wonderment. *Salauds!* he mumbles under his breath.

Louise is on her feet, a furious expression on her face. Edouard is behind her. "You are going to do nothing?" she says, coming toward René. Her heavy steps on the lobby floor resound. "You are not going to do anything about that Arabic burka girl?"

"You have it wrong, Louise," I say. "You are speaking of Lilith. Don't refer to her that way." I am angry. Louise turns and glares at me.

"Madame Croix," René says. "There is nothing illegal in what Lilith is doing—not in this country. What do you expect?"

"I expect some sort of justice. That Lilith is a disgrace to her father…"

"Well let that Boudi fellow—or whatever his name is—deal with it. It's his daughter, after all—not yours."

Louise grabs Edouard's coat sleeve and drags him forward out the door. Oh these irate women, I think, a vision of Sylvie doing the same to Dr. Paxière, literally pulling him out of the restaurant, *Pain et Chocolat.*

René comes over to where I am standing next to Brit.

"And you, Madame Elizabeth. You are involved in all this Lilith business, no?"

I gulp. "Well, I guess…sort of."

"That old brown coat? Yours?"

I nod. "It's not that old."

"The red mittens?"

I nod again.

"You gave her a disguise, no? I understand from Monsieur," he says, glancing over at Jean-Luc, "that you kept her burka in your room."

"Once he kept it in his office—didn't you Jean-Luc?"

"Once," he says softly.

"Well, the father of our little renegade guest of The Majestic—Monsieur Boudi, apparently is in a rage. He wants to sue the Hotel Marcel for harboring her."

At this, Jean-Luc claps both hands against both his cheeks. *"Mon Dieu!"* escapes him.

"Oh, don't worry, Jean-Luc," René assures him. "What could possibly be the charges? Being hospitable to the girl? Please. A law suit would be a joke!" Jean-Luc looks visibly relieved.

My God! I think. At least there has been no mention of Duke Pierre Davis.

If 'big-daddy' learned of the young African-American's passion for Lilith—a passion reciprocated, I might add—who knows what major mischief might fall upon all of us. With his hired thugs and pots of money, the emir was someone for all of us to fear.

Above all others, Lilith.

CHAPTER TWENTY-SIX

Explosion

IT HAD TO happen. And it started at dawn.

I am awakening on this Saturday morning to a sleeting rain that taps on the French doors to the balcony, tick, tick, tick. Above this repetitive little annoyance, I hear the sound of a male voice, deep, loud, and angry. It comes from outside and to the right of my building. I know of a certain who owns that voice that shouts in Arabic. It is Lilith's father, Hamad al-Boudi.

Beneath this combustible sound, I hear the noise of weeping, a moaning wail that only a woman can produce. It is a young voice, this crying, uncontrollable and so sad. I hear her mumbled words, in Arabic, sorrowful, repentant, and numb with fear. I also hear another female voice, more even and resolute, perhaps Lilith's mother or one of her 'aunts.'

The sounds are loud, even though the balcony doors to Lilith's luxury suite on the fifth floor of The Majestic are firmly shut. By now, I am out on my own balcony in the dark before sunrise, in a terrycloth robe with a towel over my head against the sleet. In the open air, the sound grows louder, increases, the voices overlapping in a kind of terrible music. After many minutes, I hear a door slam shut, but the moaning sobs of a young girl continue, growing dimmer and dimmer until they cease altogether.

I return to my bed, chilled to the heart. I cannot sleep again. I can only imagine what the consequences are to be for Lilith, my little friend, with her dreams of a life of freedom quashed, and the burka enclosing her body and her hope.

As the morning deepens, and faint rays of the sun enter my room through the balcony glass doors, I rise to dress. It is wet on the balcony, as I step outside, binoculars in hand. Across the street, I see Duke's anxious face as he peers from the upper part of his attic door. He is gazing at The Majestic balcony, fifth floor. There is no one there.

It is near 10:00 AM when I see below, Lilith emerge from the entrance door to The Majestic Hotel. She is in full burka, face veiled, hair covered. Each arm is held by a bodyguard, one of whom I recognize. Ahmed. Her little figure droops, shoulders down, head lowered as she is physically placed in the seat of a waiting white stretch limousine. At no time, in her walk to the curb, has she looked up toward me nor across the avenue to the attic room of apartment building 2. Banished from Paris, she disappears from view as the limousine pulls away from the curb and into traffic.

With my binoculars, I look at Duke. His face has an expression of such despair, it brings tears to my eyes as I see him slowly shut the attic door, his Lilith gone.

I am distraught by this turn of events, yet realize it was in the cards, that there was no way the liaison between Duke and Lilith could possibly be viable for any length of time. And the emir? I doubt he even knew about the existence of an African American youth, named Duke Pierre Davis, much less that his daughter was listening to his music in a nightspot called *Le Club*.

Wow! I'd hate to hear the fall-out if ever he discovered their loving connection.

I decide to go downstairs, dispirited though I may be. As I start to enter the salon for a late *café au lait, croissant,* and jam, Brigitte, on duty at the desk on week-ends, calls me over.

"This is left for you, Madame Elizabeth." She hands me an envelope.

"When did this come?"

"A lady…an Arab lady…appeared with it very early…I believe before 8:00 o'clock."

"A young Arab lady," I ask? "Was she young?"

"No. I don't think so. It is hard to tell…you know…with that…"

"Burka," I interject.

"Yes. Also she was quite heavy. I have seen the young one…it was not her."

"Thank you Brigitte," and I walk away as she goes back to the kitchenette to fix my breakfast.

At the table, I open the envelope. There is a folded piece of paper marked Elizabeth. There is a second smaller envelope addressed to Duke in Lilith's delicate handwriting. I unfold my note from her:

'Dear Elizabeth: You have been so kind to me. Thank you for the use of your coat and mittens. I can never believe how you helped make possible the joy I discovered in Paris. I will never forget. If I should ever see you again, I will embrace you as my true friend. Lilith. Please give this envelope to my Duke.'

Breakfast arrives. I can hardly pour the coffee nor taste a piece of *croissant* because there seem to be tears in my throat. All I can think of is my tender Romeo/Juliet romance split asunder, and the pain the two must feel.

CHAPTER TWENTY-SEVEN

A Crowded Lobby

AFTER A DESULTORY breakfast, later in the morning, I sit perusing The International New York Times, left on the lounge coffee table for patrons of the Hotel Marcel to read. Then secretively, I begin doing the crossword puzzle in pen. I know it is not polite, but I am trying to distract myself. I do not want to return to my room, the thought too depressing.

As I sit there, I see Nelson, the manager of The Majestic, enter the lobby and approach Brigitte at the check-in desk.

"Monsieur Marcel," he says. *"Je veux parler avec lui."* His French pronunciation is horrible.

"Il n'est pas ici les week-ends," Brigitte responds, at which Nelson wrings his hands. "I must leave him a message," he continues in English, with strong British accent. "Give me a pen, please." Brigitte hands him one and a note pad on which he scribbles hastily, and I can see, in very large letters. He hands the note to Brigitte.

"And you'd best tell Monsieur Marcel that it is imperative he come to

The Majestic and see the sheikh who demands an audience. It is absolutely necessary or there will be big trouble for this...this establishment!"

Nelson looks around disdainfully, just as I notice Doctor Guillaume Paxière appear in the doorway.

Oh, God. Not him again, but it is he and he makes his way directly over to me and sits beside me on the sofa.

"Elizabeth."

This Saturday is turning into a nightmare before my eyes. I am to meet Brit for dinner tomorrow at *La Cocotte*. It has become 'our' place. Thankfully, there is that in my future, but the here and now is dismal. I let out a sigh.

"Who is that British gentleman?" the doctor asks. "He certainly seems angry."

"He's the manager from the hotel next door."

"Seems an unpleasant fellow. Ah, there he goes," and in saying this, I find the doctor's hand on my knee.

"Oh, please, Guillaume, grow up!" and I brush his hand away, just as I see Elise Frontenac rush into the hotel. She is dressed in a chic, expensive gray coat. Her legs—which I had never noticed before—are long and lovely, and I notice that Guillaume is busy taking them in. Elise sees me in the lounge and rushes toward me.

"Elizabeth, I must speak with you. Excuse me, Monsieur..."

Guillaume rises, as do I. "I am Doctor Paxière, Madame...?"

"Frontenac," Elise says, blushing.

"*Enchanté,*" the doctor says, leaning to kiss her gloved hand.

"Come along, Elise," I say, skirting this little flirtation, and I take her by the arm to the rear of the salon, leaving Guillaume disconcerted. "What is it?"

"It's Duke."

"Oh, no."

"Yes. He came to the apartment around noon, so upset. I have never seen him like that. He was actually crying, tears running down his face, wetting his shirt collar. The poor boy was...how you say...outside himself."

"Beside himself," I correct her.

"Yes. Yes. You know him well and he is fond of you. Can you do anything to help him? I'm not quite sure what's going on with him. Do you know?"

"Well. Yes," I say. "I have a pretty good idea. Tell him to come see me, would you? Perhaps I can help."

"Is it all right this afternoon? He's still sitting sadly with Pierre...you know, father and son," and Elise smiles bleakly.

"I'm glad your husband is there for him. But do tell him to come over this afternoon. Right now, if he wishes."

She nods, goes to the lobby, past Guillaume Paxière who is standing at attention.

"*Au revoir, Docteur,*" she says, with a simper. "*Absolument,*" is his reply. Good Lord, I think. There is no stopping him, is there?

"Elise," I say. "Tell Duke to go the desk and call my room upstairs. I will be waiting there for him."

"Of course." And she leaves. I give a cheery wave to Doctor Paxière. "Keep up the good work," I say facetiously, at which he looks bewildered, having no idea what I mean, and I go back to the *ascenseur*. On arrival on the fifth floor, I go to my room, and sit on my bed awaiting my favorite African-American musician to come in the door and accept the letter from Lilith I now hold in my hand.

CHAPTER TWENTY-EIGHT

A Golden Key

DUKE HOLDS THE envelope for a long moment. He sinks to the coverlet on my bed as I stand beside him. Slowly he unseals it. First comes out a single page, followed by a tiny gold key, which drops into his hand all by itself.

Duke stares at it. There are no tears, but his eyes are red. He bends to read the contents of Lilith's letter. He does not speak. His shoulders sag. His head is lowered, as was hers when she left this morning.

Finally, I ask, "Are you okay?"

"He nods. "Yes, But Lilith isn't." His voice breaks.

"I know." I sit beside him on the bed. "I saw her leave this morning— being led to the waiting car by two bodyguards—one on each arm—in her burka—even a face veil. In the last couple of years in France, it is illegal to cover the face in a public place."

"It's against French law?"

"Two years ago they passed legislation called The Burka Bill. Because Lilith was probably headed via limousine, to a private jet back to Qatar, the face veil wouldn't matter. I'm sure her father forced her to wear it."

"As part of her punishment," Duke says. "I saw her too from the attic window. She didn't even dare look up. It was raining," he says as a sad afterthought.

Duke rises, paces in the small room. He holds the key tightly in his hand. "It's not over. It'll never be over," he says grimly.

"Oh, Duke, my dear." I am at a loss for words.

"You don't understand, Elizabeth," Duke declares vehemently. "We are pledged to each other." Then, shaking her letter in my face, as I had shaken Lilith's picture under Ray's nose, Duke says, "She wants to come back. She says she has to come back to me. I've told her more than once that I'd find her no matter what."

Then, with the other hand, a fist holding the golden key, he continues, "This is a code. She knows I will find her, and she will know I am there when I return this to her. She wears its chain around her neck." His voice holds more confidence as he speaks. "Even secretly. Even over the garden wall. Even under the eyes of bodyguards. I will have her back."

"Oh, Duke."

"She's counting on it. And so am I!"

He is so adamant, he has made me believe that maybe, one day, it might be possible that they would be together. I go to the drawer in the built in desk of my room, and from it, pick up the black velvet bag that contains Sue's 'pillbox' present. I take it over to Duke who has reseated himself on the corner of my bed.

"Here," I say, presenting him with my little treasure.

"What?" He is lost in thought.

"To hold the key."

"What?" Again. At last, he takes the bag and extracts the tiny, gold, rectangular box. I show him how to pull aside the top and, taking the key from his hand, I place it inside and slide the lid over. It's a perfect fit.

Better this key than some lady's pill, no?

Duke looks at me. He smiles. "Brilliant!" he exclaims. He takes the golden box and places it in the inner pocket of his jacket.

"Elizabeth, you give me hope."

"I can't give you much else. And perhaps I shouldn't. Your quest may be impossible."

Leaping to his feet, Duke embraces me as I stand beside the bed. "I'm going to Qatar!"

"No!"

"Oh, yes. I'm going to Qatar to capture my love—even if I have to kidnap her. My Lilith. She belongs to me. And I to her."

Duke is off in a rush before I can issue another word of warning. He leaves me quaking for his safety, and for the enormity of what he undertakes. The code, the tiny key, lies securely in its coffin of gold next to his heart.

CHAPTER TWENTY-NINE

Starlight

SUNDAY MORNING, I decide to walk over to the Rodin Museum, an easy amble from the hotel, past *Les Invalides*. It is not so cold today. My infamous brown coat is more than sufficient against the chill, and I wear a new pair of boots.

It is always restorative for me to go to the Rodin. Housed in the château-like *L'Hôtel Biron*, where he lived and worked, Rodin's sculptures are so accessible, so close, one feels one can touch them, that they are alive. And just one hour spent there, is inspiration.

In the gardens, too, are marble figures and larger group pieces. Although it is winter, the outside landscape is perfectly kept and as one comes upon a large figure of a naked man, it seems absolutely natural for him to be there. He looks about to speak.

Brit is coming to the Hotel Marcel later this afternoon. With Jean-Luc and Isabella, we are going to invade The Majestic bar. Jean-Luc is determined to evince his right to enjoy the place, without having to bow to the will of Hamad al-Boudi, whom he has no intention of seeing.

In my little black dress, shiny new boots and diamond studs, we meet in the lobby effusively and make the short trip to the hotel next door. We find a table in the dimly–lit bar, after passing Nelson at the entrance desk, Jean-Luc giving him a nod of hello and a big smile.

At the table, over wine, I ask Jean-Luc how his negotiations with Louise are progressing.

"I am pleased," he says. "We have agreed on a price…finally! She is not an easy woman to deal with."

"I should say not. Although I'm glad for you about the apartment, Louise is a problematic person," I say. "I cannot forgive her 'fingering' Lilith. It was unnecessary. It was cruel."

"I agree," Isabella chimes in. "But she will be gone in a matter of months and out of our lives."

"Hopefully," I say.

"In spite of her, I believe I will be in the duplex by May. Or I should say we," Jean-Luc says, patting Isabella's hand. "We are so eager…"

"I can't wait to decorate. I hate all that dark green furniture. I hope they take it with them to the country. It makes the place so gloomy." Isabella is speaking with excitement, which suddenly turns to a lower key, as Nelson approaches our table, from the entrance hall.

He stops beside Jean-Luc. "You have come to see Hamad al-Boudi? I see."

"No. I came to have a drink."

"Does Hamad al-Boudi expect you?"

"Look, Monsieur, I told you. I am here to have a drink with my friends."

"He demands a meeting with you."

"Let him demand away. I have no interest in meeting with him. Have him come to my office tomorrow, if he likes. I will be at the Hotel Marcel all day. You tell Boudi that."

"Hamad al-Boudi," Nelson hisses and walks away, furious.

We are all subdued for a moment. Then, Jean-Luc pipes up, "Elizabeth, who is this doctor that seems to be pursuing you? He seems to hang around…"

"Please, Jean-Luc," I say, glancing at Brit who has suddenly sat up, straightening his shoulders. "Dr. Guillaume Paxière. He's a joke. I met him five years ago. Right now he is pursuing Sylvie LaGrange, if you can believe it."

Jean-Luc throws back his head and laughs. "Sylvie?"

"He loves lonely widows with money," I say somewhat ruefully, again glancing at Brit who seems relieved with Jean-Luc's laughter.

"You should have seen him flirt with Elise Frontenac yesterday."

"I guess he finds this street ripe for the picking with you and Sylvie and Elise," continues Jean-Luc.

"But not Louise," I say with a laugh. "She's not his type."

And at that moment, Madge and Jerry, the American couple, appear in the doorway of the bar. As they pass the table, Madge says, dripping honey, "Did you see that little Arab girl leave yesterday in the rain? And what a ruckus before that…woke us up…right Jerry, honey?"

I do not reply.

"Cat got your tongue?" Jerry says, leaning down to me.

"You are nasty people," I say turning away.

With a harrumph of sorts, the two proceed to the far end of the room.

Brit, sensing my consternation, says, "Come on now. I think it's time for Elizabeth and me to get a bite to eat, don't you?" turning to me.

"*Bonne idée*," I say, as Jean-Luc calls for the bill. We collect our belongings and leave. Saying goodbye to Jean-Luc and Isabella on the street in front of Hotel Marcel, with embraces and fond farewells, Brit and I walk over to *La Terrasse*.

After cheese omelets and *tarte au citron*, we re-cross the avenue to Hotel Marcel. The night is clear and cold, the stars brilliant in a dark sky. They look enormous, touchable. They seem to match the light in my diamond studs and the glow in my lover's eyes

CHAPTER THIRTY

Not Your Normal Monday

I AM AT my usual breakfast post in the salon. It is near 9:00 o'clock this Monday morning. Just as I take the last sip of *café au lait*, Nelson from the hotel next door appears. He approaches Jean-Luc who sits behind the entrance desk, going over accounts.

"Monsieur," he says to Jean-Luc. "Hamad al-Boudi wishes you to come to The Majestic and speak with him."

"About what?" Jean-Luc replies mildly.

"It is a personal matter."

"Well, then, as I told you last night, have him drop by. I'll see him in my office," and Jean-Luc points with a finger to the back of the building. (That cluttered space? I can't imagine the confrontation.)

"Hmm." Nelson seems nonplussed. "That is not acceptable. Hamad al-Boudi expects you to come to his suite on the fifth floor."

"Not going to happen. Monsieur Nelson, I am a busy man. If the gentleman wishes to see me I am afraid he will have to come here." And with that, Jean-Luc snaps shut his account book definitively.

Nelson looks uncomfortable. He pauses for a moment. "I will report your message," he mutters and leaves the building hurriedly.

I go up to my room and call Sue. We make a date for lunch at our usual haunt for Wednesday. It suddenly dawns upon me that is my next to last day, that I leave Paris for New York City on Friday. I have been so absorbed in all the drama that the thought comes as something of a shock.

I next walk to the nearby stationary-cum-souvenir shop and purchase a number of small gifts for friends—two handsome writing pens, a box of notepaper with Paris scenes, three Post-it boxes with pictures of the Étoile and the Bois de Boulogne. Later in the week, I will purchase gift boxes of macaroons at *Le Nôtre* for friends who have developed a taste for them and have come to expect me to bring them this sweet gift.

I stop for a bite at *Pain et Chocolat,* another ham on *baguette,* so delicious. No sign of the good doctor, thank goodness. Purchases in hand, I return to Hotel Marcel to find René Poignal chatting with Jean-Luc who is at his desk.

The two men greet me with enthusiasm.

"Ah, Madam," the policeman says with a smile, "Are you in any more trouble today."

"No more than yesterday," I say with a little laugh. As we parlay our little word game, we are interrupted by the entrance of a big man, over six feet tall. In his robes, emitting a surge of energy, Hamad al-Boudi enters the lobby of Hotel Marcel, seeming to suck up all the air in the small space.

Accompanying him is bodyguard, Ahmed.

Hamad al-Boudi stands squarely in front of Jean-Luc who remains seated. Rene turns and moves into the back hall. I am alone by the staircase leading to the basement area.

Jean-Luc looks up. He is completely calm. "Monsieur?" He pretends he has no idea who this person is.

Ahmed responds formally. "This is Hamad al-Boudi, Monsieur Marcel."

"Can't he speak for himself?"

"I am his interpreter," Ahmed continues. "He knows some English but little French."

"*Eh bien,* what is it he wants?"

I wait with bated breath. This is too rich a confrontation to miss!

"Monsieur," Hamad al-Boudi booms forth. His voice is deep, forbidding. "It is my daughter I want to…" and he looks at Ahmed.

"He wants to discuss his daughter and the fact that you—in this hotel—gave her a place to disgrace herself by divesting herself of her burka and flouncing around the city shamelessly."

"I did what?" Jean-Luc remarks.

"You heard me. We know this is true from the word of the wife of the once French Ambassador to Ethiopia, who lives across the street. She informed the manager of The Majestic, a Monsieur Nelson, of the fact."

Our little friend, Louise Croix.

"This is ridiculous," says Jean-Luc, rising to his feet. He directs his words to Ahmed. "His daughter came into the hotel last week and asked to use the lavatory."

Ahmed translates this to his boss who turns red.

"Ask him if I should have said no?" Jean-Luc continues. "She was most polite. I obliged her."

Suddenly, Hamad al-Boudi says in a loud voice, "I buy this hotel."

Jean-Luc gives a dry laugh.

"I put you out of business!"

"I don't think so," says Jean-Luc.

"This…dirty little place…" Hamad al-Boudi is sputtering.

"What do you call dirty," Jean-Luc is angry.

"Then, al-Boudi shouts, "I'll sue!" His eyes are aflame.

At this moment, from the back hall and around the corner of the desk, saunters René Poignal. He approaches Hamad al-Boudi, shows him his badge, and asks him, "On what grounds would you sue Hotel Marcel?"

Hamad al-Boudi looks confused for a moment, turns to Ahmed, who responds to René with the words, "He," pointing at Jean-Luc, "he is responsible for allowing the daughter to go about Paris in the disguise of an old brown coat and red gloves, permitting her…"

"There is no illegality here at all, Ahmed. Tell your master that there is no law suit possible because Monsieur Marcel has committed no crime."

"He ruins my daughter," Hamad al-Boudi says, his voice ringing.

"How so? To let her go around Paris in the dress of Europeans? I don't think that is criminal in anyone's country and certainly not in France. No, Monsieur," and here, René addresses Hamad al-Boudi directly. "Sir. You are not a diplomat. You are a businessman from Qatar, here in the capital on vacation with your family. You have no diplomatic immunity."

Then René gets really serious. He moves close to the man, dwarfed by him, yet the stronger of the two. "If anything—anything at all—goes amiss in this hotel—if something should happen to the property or to any person here, I can and will charge you with harassment." René turns away with a flourish, then swings back. "And you can count on it being in all of the papers!"

Bravo, René, I think. I see Hamad al-Boudi disappear in a flurry of robes, followed by Ahmed with his head down, running after him.

CHAPTER THIRTY-ONE

The Cover of French Vogue

SASHA TAPS ON my door on Tuesday morning and invites me to lunch.

"Are you free?" he asks as I open my door in my terrycloth robe.

"What time is it?" I am somewhat disoriented with sleep.

"It's 9:30," he says looking at his watch. "Ray Guild and I are going over to *Le Copain*. It is famous for the *coq au vin*—which I am craving. I know you're leaving Friday, and he and I want to take you to a farewell lunch."

"Sounds lovely. Of course I'll come."

"Ray will pick us up here in his car—an old American Chevrolet—not very chic."

"Who cares? if it runs," I say. "I guess, Sasha, you have no one any longer to photograph on the next balcony, with Lilith gone."

"You're wrong," he replies with a delighted smile. "Yesterday, I got a picture of the old man in his Arab outfit, smoking a cigar. It is a wonderful picture—The Eiffel Tower in the background –the smoke in the air."

"He was out there—on her balcony?"

"Yep." Sasha returns to his room next to mine.

Later, as planned, Ray appears around noon in a gray, rundown looking vehicle. We clamber in and cross the d'Iena Bridge to the Right Bank. *Le Copain* is on a side street off of avenue Montaigne. Ray is able to park in front of the entrance to the restaurant.

The place is charming, with pink tablecloths and pale green walls. It is not large, but as we are early, there is no problem finding a table near the window looking out at the street. Of course, we order wine. It arrives with a small plate of *amuse bouches*, tiny cheese *gougères*, and slivers of salami each with its own toothpick. The main event for all three of us is the *coq au vin*, and it is truly a spectacular dish.

"How did Hamad al-Boudi look, on the balcony yesterday," I ask Sasha.

"What do you mean?"

"Well he was in such a rage earlier, at the Hotel, threatening to sue Jean-Luc for corrupting his daughter, I thought he might have looked— oh, I don't know—upset, maybe, sad, maybe—you know he banished Lilith in disgrace."

"I know," says Sasha. I was witness."

"Me too," I add.

"She left already?" asks Ray.

"Yep. She's gone—off to Qatar in full burka—face-veil and all."

"No!" Ray is surprised.

We are demolishing the succulent chicken down to the bones. The sauce is so seductive, the three of us are busy dunking chunks of *baguette* into its depths.

Finally, I decide I have to bring up the fate of the photograph of Lilith at The Eiffel Tower.

"You can't use it," I say softly to Ray.

"Can't use what?" he replies.

"You know what I'm talking about! The picture."

"Why not? Why can't we use it? Lilith is gone. It can't cause her any more trouble, now can it?"

"Are you kidding, Ray? Of course it can. It could put her in grave danger."

"Now, Elizabeth," Sasha chimes in. "Let's not get carried away. She's in Qatar. Her father will be back there before the *Vogue* issue comes out. He'll never see it."

"You don't think *Vogue* is on the newsstands in Qatar? Doha, its capital, is a very wealthy city—all that oil—and did you happen to notice that Hamad al-Boudi's women managed to go to Victoria's Secret to shop? These people are not unsophisticated!" I am angry at both of my friends' lack of sense on the matter.

"Aw, Elizabeth," both Ray and Sasha are saying, patting my hand as if I were a child. "Don't get so upset. It's just a picture," Sasha adds.

"Yes," I say, "a picture that could put that girl in jeopardy." The chicken has turned to ashes in my mouth.

"Look," says Ray, very businesslike. "We are going to use the picture."

"But…" I interject.

"But," he continues. "We will not put the name of the model anywhere in the credits. She will be anonymous. I promise you. That should take care of things. No one will have any idea who she is."

"Except maybe her father!" I say.

Sasha then puts the *coup de grâce* to the whole idea of Lilith's privacy.

"I have to be honest with you, Elizabeth. I am going to use one of the photographs of Lilith at The Eiffel Tower—a slightly different picture, taken at the same shoot—not the one for *Vogue*—well, I am going to put it in my new book *Les Façades de Paris*. It is just too fine an image not to."

I say no more this lunch. I sit as the two men gobble down *crèmes brûlées*. I can't even touch the dark coffee that follows. They know I am upset. They may even feel some guilt about Lilith, but they are joking and laughing, as if nothing had transpired, their jollity only another kind of *façade* in evidence.

CHAPTER THIRTY-ONE

The Final Bead of Caviar

IN A DOWNCAST mood, I meet with Sue on our regular banquette at *Caviar Kaspia*. This Wednesday, I am more interested in the vodka than the sturgeon delight –unusual indeed for me.

"You seem low, sweetheart," Sue pronounces. "What's the matter? It's not Brit?"

"No. No. He is wonderful." I point out the diamond studs I am wearing. "A New Year's present."

"Lovely," Sue says. "I'm so glad you two are on track."

"We are. Very much so. I plan to come back to Paris in May, and Brit is coming to New York for the whole summer," I say, my frame of mind lightening considerably at the thought.

"Terrific. But then, what is bothering you? I know there's something."

"It's about Lilith. Oh, Sue, I am so worried for her. Her father—a truly frightening, enormous fellow, came to the Hotel Marcel and threatened to sue Jean-Luc for harboring his daughter. Of course, according to the policeman, Poignal, he has no case. But Hamad al-Boudi…"

"Hamad al-Boudi? That's his name?"

I nod. "He was in a rage. The day before, at dawn, I heard him—from the hotel next door—literally—shrieking at his daughter in Arabic, of course. I could hear Lilith crying, poor little girl, and the next thing I know, midmorning, I see her leaving the hotel in full burka regalia—headed back to Qatar presumably. It was awful. She could barely get into the limo."

"You think she was beaten?" Sue looks horrified.

"No. I really don't. I think she was so disheartened, she could hardly walk."

Then, I tell Sue of my lunch with Sasha and Ray and their decision to use the picture of Lilith at The Eiffel Tower for *Vogue's* next edition. I told her how dangerous I thought it was for Lilith, and that Sasha was going to use a similar picture in his book, *Les Façades de Paris.*

"Oh Lord," says Sue. "That book could be circulated around the civilized world—even in good old Qatar."

"I know."

The two of us have already consumed a carafe of vodka (a small carafe.)

"I think we had better order," says Sue, which we do. I have the poached eggs –*Diaghilev*—with caviar on top; she orders smoked salmon with toast points. And of course, we request a second (small) carafe of the cold vodka.

We eat in silence. Sue says, finally, "You _are_ coming back to Paris in May, aren't you? I do miss you."

"Yes. I plan to. Brit is expecting me," I say with a smile. "Also, I think by then, Jean-Luc and Isabella will be living across the street in the Croix apartment. He tells me that he and Louise—that awful woman—you know, it was she that reported Lilith's running around Paris without her burka—she who told the manager of The Majestic and one of the bodyguards—she who got Lilith in all that trouble—I hate her..."

"I know you do...can't blame you. But tell me, did Jean-Luc really buy the duplex?"

"He says they have a deal," I say, calming down.

"How about that doctor you were telling me about?"

"Oh, he's around on the street looking for prey. I think he is now after Elise Frontenac."

No."

"Yes. He certainly was flirting with her—and she didn't seem to mind at all. He's really kind of sleazy."

"I would say so…And Duke?"

"He is beside himself at losing Lilith—at least her presence." And I proceed to tell Sue of the golden pillbox she had given me, now the coffin of the tiny key that will bring Lilith back to Duke. "I hope you don't mind. It seemed such a good cause."

"Of course not. It was yours to do with what you wished. And what a romantic ending. What a useful purpose for that little box. I hope it works."

"I do too."

We sit for some time, finishing the last drops of vodka, and for me, the last bead of caviar. It is a delicious moment of two old friends communing. It is the final repast we share until spring comes to Paris, and I, along with it. There is nothing sad about our goodbye for we will meet again, God willing, when the chestnut trees are in bloom and Paris smells of the sweetness of spring. Already, I can't wait.

CHAPTER THIRTY-TWO

"We'll Meet Again"

IT IS MY very last night in Paris and I spend it with Brit. All night.

We dine at *La Cocotte*, sitting close by the fire, with the roast chicken before us, delectably golden and aromatic. Neither of us can eat a bite. We gaze at each other, memorizing lines and profiles, chin structure and the shape of lips. We speak little.

It is absolutely incumbent on me to go this night of nights to *Le Club*. I not only want to hear Duke Pierre Davis and his fine music, but I must see him, test his determination, and wish him God speed. Brit seems as invested as I in Duke's pursuit of love. My lover is as romantic as I.

It is not late when we reach *Le Club*. In fact, the band is only in the middle of the first set. It is jazzy and hot, melodies of the 1950s, swing music of the big bands of the era. Duke plays well, but automatically, as if his head is in another place. And his heart.

At the break, he notices Brit and me at a little table in the corner. He comes to join us and sits for the 15 minutes allowed before the second set.

"Are you okay?" I inquire.

"Better than that," he responds.

"Have you made any decisions?" My questions are tentative.

"All I know is I'm going to Qatar."

"No, Duke. Really?" I let out a small gasp.

"Yes, really." Duke pulls from his pocket a Qater Airline ticket, one way, to the Hamad International Airport in Doha, the capital of Qatar, dated two days hence.

I am speechless. Brit asks him, "You're sure about this?"

Duke responds, "Absolutely. I am taking a leave. I can come back here, always, they told me if not on bass if they've hired another bassist, but for my violin. I have been assured—so I'm confident in going."

"What does your father—Pierre Frontenac think of this? And Elise?" I ask.

"Of course, they are upset…they think I'm crazy. But at least father knows what it's like to be…obsessed with love," and Duke beams a smile so compelling, both Brit and I have to smile back.

"Gotta' go," says Duke, rising. "We're on again," and he moves to the small stage and takes his place on it.

The quartet, Duke on bass, begins with a slow, rendering of the song, "But Not For Me." I watch his face. It is as sad as the music itself. When they finish, Duke sets aside his bass, picks up the violin on a chair adjacent to the stone wall, and starts on a throbbing, piercing version of "Unforgettable," made famous by Nat King Cole. This time, I see tears in the young man's eyes.

Brit looks at me with a look of love he can't disguise, a look I return in kind. We hold hands as the lovely rendering of the song, the sweet high string notes from Duke's violin filling the room. Nobody in the audience makes a sound.

Until the end, when rousing applause takes over the room.

We decide to leave, eager to be alone. Duke is free again and I beckon him over to the table and pour him a glass of wine. He sits with us. I still see tears in his eyes but they do not fall. I tell him how I hope to see him in the spring, with Brit at my side, and for him to let Jean-Luc know where he is, if he's back in Paris at *Le Club*.

"I don't want to lose you, Duke. I also want to know so much what happens for you with Lilith. She is so lovely," and Duke interrupts, with "Oh yes, that she is. That she is, and when I get there, remember, I have the key in its little gold box." He pats the left breast pocket of his jacket. "Somehow I'll get it to her."

As he returns to the stage to his work, we get up to leave. I hug him and say, "I love you, Duke." He hugs me tighter, and breathes a soft, "Me too."

Brit claps him on the shoulder and says, "Go get your girl!" at which Duke beams, and nods his head vigorously. We wait until he's on the stage, back on his bass, and playing "We'll Meet Again, Don't know where, Don't know when," the music haunting and melancholy, our exit from *Le Club*.

The rest of the night is spent in my room, back at Hotel Marcel. It is the blur of a lover's goodbye. The next morning, Brit brings me to the de Gaulle airport in his Peugeot. He leaves me at check-in, with a lingering kiss and the soft words, "We'll meet again, darling. No doubt of it," and he's gone before I have the chance to answer. We'll meet again. I know where. I know when.

In Paris. In the month May.

EPILOGUE

THE PLANE IS full. We take off in the great whoosh that lifts the stomach and questions the heart. As I settle back into the narrow, uncomfortable seat, my mind is still on the ground, in Paris, and in his arms.

Yet, I leave with so many unanswered enigmas, problems unsolved, dreams to be fulfilled.

Brit, of course, not a problem but a dream to complete.

And Marianna's mother. Will I ever see her again? I liked her.

Duke in Qatar. Will Hamad al-Boudi harm him? Will Lilith be able to join with her young lover? Her photograph? Sasha and Ray? Will they keep her anonymous? Will they really place her in the awfully exposed position, the cover of French *Vogue?* What will become of her if her father sees it? I fear for her. And Sasha's book, *Les Façades de Paris?*

Will Jean-Luc and Isabella be ensconced in the Croix apartment in May? What fun it would be to see them there, to view the new decor Isabella provides. Will there perhaps be a marriage in the spring? How delicious that would be! And how Jean-Luc will enjoy overseeing Hotel Marcel from across the avenue. How well he can observe his nemesis,

The Majestic, from his new vantage point, and conduct the war between the two hotels from a distance.

Will Doctor Paxière continue to bed Sylvie LaGrange? Or will he have moved a short way down the street to Elise Frontenac's boudoir? And what of Elise's husband, Pierre? How would he be able to accept that little outcome?

I hope fervently that on my return, old Madge and Jerry are long gone, back to their cheese grits and ham hocks in Alabama where they belong. I learned from Jean-Luc, that Jerry owns four fast food franchises and has a sack of money (probably under a mattress somewhere in that Southern state.)

I hope too that Louise Croix and her poor, benighted husband are safely out-of-town in the Forest of Fontainebleau, lost in the woods permanently. I can never forgive her betrayal of Lilith, and what is more, her obvious relish in doing so. *Quelle chienne!*

Then, there is my sweet Sue, friends forever, she and I. We understand each other so well. She is my sounding board, her generous wisdom and her affection true.

I decide to write to Brit. I pull down the tabletop from the back seat of the passenger in front of me and compose a very brief line to Brit, telling him of my joy in finding such a companion and lover as he. I also express my concern for the small hotel, Hotel Marcel, and the fear that Jean-Luc may lose his battle against the giant Majestic that looms over the street and could swallow him up.

God help Jean-Luc, I write to Brit, and God help me too, for I find my identity there in that small establishment on the Left Bank. Near the Invalides and the Rodin Museum, The Eiffel Tower as beacon to follow, Hotel Marcel is a place where the spirit of Paris reigns supreme.

And what a spirit it is!

Bien sûr.